MW00914566

SCATTERED
SOULS

SCATTERED
SOULS

Shahnaz Bashir

First published in India in 2016 by Fourth Estate
An imprint of HarperCollins *Publishers*

Copyright © Shahnaz Bashir 2016

P-ISBN: 978-93-5264-124-6
E-ISBN: 978-93-5264-125-3

2 4 6 8 10 9 7 5 3 1

Shahnaz Bashir asserts the moral right
to be identified as the author of this work.

HarperCollins *Publishers*
A-75, Sector 57, Noida, Uttar Pradesh 201301, India
1 London Bridge Street, London, SE1 9GF, United Kingdom
Hazelton Lanes, 55 Avenue Road, Suite 2900, Toronto, Ontario M5R 3L2
and 1995 Markham Road, Scarborough, Ontario M1B 5M8, Canada
25 Ryde Road, Pymble, Sydney, NSW 2073, Australia
195 Broadway, New York, NY 10007, USA

Typeset in 16/16 Adobe Arabic
by Jojy Philip, New Delhi

Printed and bound at
Replika Press Pvt. Ltd.

For
Shahaan Ahmad
who was born alongside this book

Contents

The Transistor

There are two ways to be fooled. One is to believe what isn't true; the other is to refuse to believe what is true.

—Søren Kierkegaard

We're all islands shouting lies to each other across seas of misunderstanding.
—Rudyard Kipling, *The Light That Failed*

If it's wrong when they do it, it's wrong when we do it.

—Noam Chomsky

Ignorance and impetuosity are inseparable twins as are rumours and misunderstandings—all fused at their heads.

With each bullet pumped into him, all his great memories of loyalty to the revolution flashed through his mind ... *Aggressively thrusting up his hand in response to the slogans of freedom ... fiercely thundering out the word* Azaadi ... *smoking cigarettes and cracking jokes with insurgents ... marching beside them in processions ... hiding them in his attic during the crackdowns ... helping them transport their weapons under his pheran ...*

risking himself by shielding them during Army raids on the village ... All done at the cost of upsetting his elder brother every now and again.

One bullet pierced the transistor along its metre-band, exploding the radio into fragments and splinters. Its remains, a soldered electronic chip connected to a naked speaker by a thin wire, lay scattered beside him, still blaring the BBC news.

As Yousuf collapsed, a tear filmed and glistened at the corner of his right eye. It glinted, waiting to fall until life fled from his eyes.

※

Muhammad Yousuf Dar was consumed by his farming engagements. His elder brother, Abdul Rahmaan Dar, was a mainstream politician greatly despised for his anti-freedom-movement position in Daddgaam. Despite their ideological differences, the two brothers lived together in their ancestral house and loved each other. They never discussed politics, nor did they speak publicly against each other.

As insurgency in Kashmir reached its peak in the early years of the 1990s, Rahmaan felt threatened. The insurgents were punishing those disloyal to the freedom movement. Consequently, Rahmaan gathered his family and migrated to Delhi, hoping to return during a respite in the troubles. Muhammad Yousuf felt very lonely without his brother and his family. He missed his nephew and niece sorely. The big ancestral house looked empty and abandoned now. Yousuf's wife and their two sons didn't make enough noise for him to be at peace. Commotion, Yousuf thought, was the symbol of well-being in the house.

Muhammad Yousuf was a man of few words. He was very fond of the radio. He listened to BBC News because he did not trust the government news reports on the conflict in Kashmir. His second favourite thing on the transistor was cricket commentary. It was almost impossible for him to miss a daily news bulletin. After years of practice, he had learnt to tune into programmes without even checking the time or schedule. Despite the static at each slight turn of the dial on the transistor, he was adept at catching the BBC signal. Even with the noisy TV playing in the room, the transistor was never silent or turned off.

He remembered the number of transistors he had cherished, changing them when they fell from ledges or slipped from the crooks of apple trees in the orchard or got damaged when the children toyed with them, or when they were ruined by leaking batteries. He had gifted some to his insurgent friends. His bedroom was a museum of old transistors. He had a collection of defunct, antique Murphy, Panasonic, Philips, Sony, Zeenat and other cardboard-framed or plastic-framed transistors, some of them clad in perforated tan or black leather encasements. The oldest was a souvenir from his

grandfather, a part-wooden and part-plastic graceful
Murphy set, the size of a plum crate. The most modern
one was a medium-sized Philips set—rickety after it had
fallen from a high shelf in the kitchen. Yousuf's wife
Naseema had unknowingly swept it off while groping
for a matchbox during a sudden power cut. Later, Yousuf
had fixed it with strips of white tape.

The first time he visited the family orchard after his
brother's migration to Delhi, Yousuf noticed that the
village regarded him strangely. It was an early spring
morning and he ambled down the Daddgaam market,
passing by the prominent Malik General Store of
Nazir Ahmad Malik. Malik was widely known by his
epithetic second name Tout'a, which meant 'parrot'. He
had a round face and his tobacco-blackened buckteeth
protruded from his lips. This made him look as though
he were constantly smiling. The village children mistook
him for a magnanimous shopkeeper because even when
he ridiculed them for asking for free candy sometimes,
he seemed to smile. The front of the shop was always
crowded with hankering, squatting, smoking and idling
village elders, endlessly gossiping about local politics.
Malik was a known scandalmonger, but some village
elders ignored this side of his personality and instead
willingly bought into everything he said wholeheartedly.
One of the idlers at Malik's shopfront was Abdul Ahad

Magray, the bearded village head who had taken a number of favours from Abdul Rahmaan Dar, and would steer the gossip towards mainstream politics. Then the bristle-cheeked Abdul Aziz Ganie, who had always been a staunch opponent of the armed movement in Daddgaam before his daughter's love marriage to a local insurgent commander, would raise his flawed arguments in favour of the armed resistance. Following them, the condescending Muhammad Ramzaan Naik, the wood trader, would make it a point to start his next comment before giving others a chance to respond to his previous one. Finally the scraggly-bearded Molvi Ali Muhammad Shah, imam of the Daddgaam Jamia Mosque, would be the last to join in, quietly listening to various views on the topic already under discussion. To any stranger approaching the shop, he would appear to be the only wise person in the group, waiting for the right time to decimate all the comments and arguments made by the others. But Molvi Shah usually tossed in the most stupid assertion and disillusioned the spectator quickly.

On that morning, Muhammad Yousuf Dar passed by Malik General Store with the transistor playing under his pheran. Malik quietly diverted the attention of the men at the shop to Yousuf. For the whole day, then, the village elders discussed the exile of Abdul Rahmaan Dar, comparing him to his younger brother, subtly criticizing the people in Kashmir who did not stand by the armed movement. Once Abdul Rahmaan had refused to help Malik's only son Altaf, a class ten dropout, get a government job. Since then Malik had been cross with the Dars.

※

A rutted and pitted main road slithered through Daddgaam, dividing it into two parts: an upper part and a lower part. The upper part was a plateau where all the apple and plum orchards were situated; the lower part was a not-so-congested residential area for the village inhabitants, large yet unplastered brick houses with open compounds, strewn with snot-nosed children, cattle, cow dung, pellets, straw, old bicycles, drying red chillies, mortars and pestles. The rest of the inhabited spaces of the village were filled with lofty walnut trees, and the market lined either side of the main road.

There was a large Army camp on the other side of the plateau, just beside the Dars' apple orchard. The Dar orchard was an ancestral property shared between Yousuf and Rahmaan. The two brothers had never properly demarcated their shares. The orchard had a barbed-wire fence along its boundary; but inside, the brothers had maintained it as if it belonged to a single owner. There was a long ridge that ran through the orchard in the middle, dividing it into two roughly equal parts. Both the brothers would attend equally to the entire orchard. Both would take their turns at pruning or spraying pesticides. Both would share the income from the annual harvest.

The Army camp was already creeping into Rahmaan

Dar's side of the orchard. Earlier the troops had been stealing apples and firewood, and now they were encroaching upon the land. They had breached the fence on one side.

The sight of four stray cows wandering about his brother's side of the orchard, trampling the ploughed ground, infuriated Muhammad Yousuf. The animals had intruded through the damaged fence. He placed his transistor in the forked crook of an apple tree, gathered his pheran on his right shoulder and began to fix the fence posts. He stretched the barbed wire. He needed a claw hammer to bend the nails on the wire. But because he had not anticipated the need, he adjusted it temporarily and filled the spaces between each tier with dry branches of bramble bush and wilted, decomposing burdocks that had lain drying along the hedge since the last summer. The hiss of the transistor alerted the troops in the camp. They quietly watched Yousuf's activity until he moved to the other side of the orchard, his own portion. There he weeded some wild hemp and hung the plants on the barbed wire.

After his migration, Rahmaan's first letter, besides enquiries about Muhammad Yousuf's and his family's well-being and many other things, asked him if he wanted anything from Delhi. Yousuf read it many times over and then, alone in his room, before stowing it in his leather vanity box, he smelled the thin blue paper of the inland letter and touched the Urdu words written with a fountain pen.

In his reply, Muhammad Yousuf wrote:

'*Everything is fine. Only the Army is advancing into the orchard, as you already know. I am worried about that. I don't really need anything, but if you can send a good transistor I'll be obliged. That is it. The one I have, the one you knew, is in bad shape. Naseema damaged it accidentally. Time and again I stuff something or the other in the battery slot to keep the batteries tightly connected. Even after repairing it twice, one or the other thing comes loose. Rest all is fine in the village ...*'

A fortnight later, a courier arrived at Muhammad Yousuf's house. He unboxed a small, bubble-wrapped transistor with its warranty card. It was a rectangular, vertically elongated, black case with two small twin grey dials on the top front. There was a tiny projection of a black antenna to its top left corner and an almost invisible metre-band strip fixed on the narrow left side. It was a transistor of a shape, colour and design he had never seen before. Yousuf filled its battery slot with new, slender batteries and turned it on. The sound it blared was loud and fresh.

❦

It was a Friday afternoon. Wielding a claw hammer in his right hand, Muhammad Yousuf Dar was bending the nails on the barbed wire in his orchard. The surroundings echoed with Friday sermons blaring from all the mosques in the village. The twelve o'clock bulletin on Yousuf's new transistor was already over and it was now just hissing in the crook of a young quince apple tree. His hands were soiled so he let it be.

As Yousuf walked towards the orchard well to wash his hands, he found Nazir Ahmad Malik standing on the dirt track outside the orchard, staring at him and the transistor. Malik was returning from his own orchard and heading to the Jamia Mosque for Friday prayers. Yousuf salaamed him and they exchanged pleasantries. Then, Malik moved on, every now and then turning to look back at Yousuf and his hissing transistor.

Once the Friday prayers were over, people burst out of the mosque door and began to huddle into small clusters on the main road. There were groups of children, adults, youths and old men—all gossiping. Nazir Ahmad Malik led his own group. As he saw Yousuf coming out of the mosque, Malik drove everyone's attention towards him. All the old men scanned Yousuf furtively. 'His brother has given him a walkie-talkie to spy on the freedom movement in the village. I saw it with my own eyes ... he was trying out the signal with the Army near his orchard.' Everyone believed what Malik said when he described Yousuf's transistor as a walkie-talkie. Malik looked sweet and composed, as always, with that smiling look on his face. Ignoring the fact that Yousuf had always stood by his own politics, the villagers instead easily connected the wrong dots.

From that Friday to the next, in the matter of a week,

the whole of Daddgaam and several other adjoining villages were abuzz with news of Yousuf's 'walkie-talkie'.

Just after his sermon, Molvi Ali Muhammad Shah announced: 'We have learnt that some unethical persons in our Daddgaam have been spying on the village. And they have been exchanging information regarding the resistance movement with the government forces through wireless sets. And yes, you heard it right: wireless sets. They have become informers and are betraying the great cause of freedom and Islam. And this announcement must serve as their last warning.'

The announcement was followed by a delay in the Friday prayers. Molvi Shah took ten more minutes to sermonize about 'betrayal and its punishment in Islam'. Yousuf listened to the announcement in awe and with great interest. He was curious and puzzled, and he wondered who those informers could be. But everyone was covertly looking at him. As Molvi Shah commenced the *khutba*, the Arabic part of the sermon, Yousuf tried to guess. His eyes wandered along the rows of worshippers. He scanned Fayaz Ahmad Bhat, an infamous boy who, the village believed, indulged in drugs. Yousuf shook his head. *No, it cannot be Fayaz; his brother Farooq sacrificed himself for the cause of freedom.* Then on his left, Yousuf found Altaf Ahmad Malik, Nazir Ahmad Malik's son, who, the people said, was the worst 'loose character' in the entire village; who had been warned several times by the insurgents to stop stalking the village girls. *No, it cannot be him either; it is not necessary that one who has a loose character would also be an informer.* Then Yousuf stopped looking around, folded his hands on his chest and concentrated on the *khutba*.

A few days later, Yousuf, as usual, was listening raptly to the 8:30 pm BBC bulletin in his kitchen. With each bit of the news about human rights' violations committed by the government forces in Kashmir, he would curse the forces under his breath. In a corner, Naseema was frying potatoes over a gas stove. Suddenly, there was a power cut. The children were writing their school homework. There came a loud bang on the main door. Yousuf and his family froze for a minute. Naseema and Yousuf looked at each other in wonder. They were not expecting any visitors at this hour, and definitely not knocking on the main door after the gate had been closed.

Then, there was another, louder knock. 'It must be the Army. They are angry with me. As I'm trying to keep them away from Brother's side of the orchard,' Yousuf whispered to Naseema. 'Don't worry. I will go and see.'

With his daring heart and shivering body, the transistor in his right hand—booming BBC—and a candle stub in the left, he went over to open the door. Yousuf placed the candle on top of the banister post opposite the main door and pulled down the bolt. In the dim candlelight, he saw three men. And before he could ask them who they were and what they wanted, they cocked their guns.

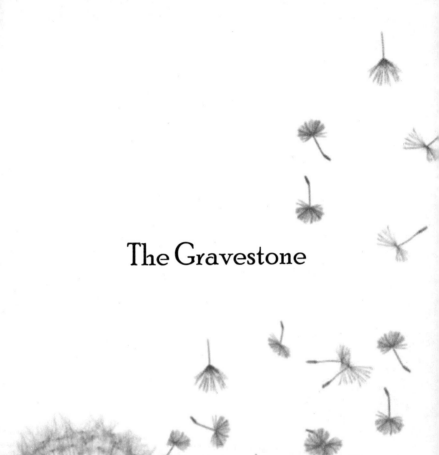

The Gravestone

A man's dying is more the survivors' affair than his own.

—Thomas Mann

All over the place, from the popular culture to the propaganda system, there is constant pressure to make people feel that they are helpless, that the only role they can have is to ratify decisions and to consume.

—Noam Chomsky

As soon as the mist lifts, he'll dash straight to the graveyard. It promises to be a really chilly evening in the wake of the April rain. He is sure the drug-addicted gamblers, for whom the graveyard is a favourite place to play whist, won't be around today.

He's scared of doing this at night. He can't sneak out in the presence of his vigilant family members. He usually goes to get his cheap Panama cigarettes from the village market in the evening. That's the time he can do it.

He lights a filterless cigarette and paces the short, narrow, flaking cement pathway outside his small mud-and-brick house. Cacti and dead geraniums, potted in discarded paint cans and small, empty Fevicol buckets, are arrayed against the walls. He finishes his cigarette, then slips back into the house, ascends the creaky wooden stairs and reaches for his old cobwebbed toolkit under the tin roof where the sloping gable makes it difficult for a grown man to stand upright. His workman's fingers are calloused, the fingertips bristly with cracks and the fingernails deformed. He rummages through the dusty tools, panting from the effort of climbing the stairs.

Shortly afterwards, he finds himself running towards the graveyard, a kilometre away from the house. The pale light of dusk falls on the asphalt road riddled with muddy puddles. The roofs and leaves still drip.

The mist is all gone and the snow-shrouded mountains appear closer than they actually are. A gust breathes through the village and shakes the groves, orchards, mustard crops and grass. Scattered plastic bags balloon into the air.

Each wrinkle and crease on his pale and weathered face tightens as he rushes on. Each strand of his grey hair stands on end. The pits in the road make him careful about where he places his plastic-shod feet. His left hand, almost dysfunctional, trembles badly. He grabs the underside of his pheran to keep the hand steady.

His worn-out pheran smells of rain and stale smoke. He scurries on. A sound of dull clanking comes from under his pheran as the rusty hammer comes into contact with the blunt chisel. Plumes of smoke-stained steam burst from his nostrils. Occasionally, a bus or a scooter passes, tooting.

Today he is welcomed again by the same stubborn clumps of nettle and thistle that are grown throughout the graveyard. And beyond—there, near the graves—are assorted irises, their stamens powdering the white petals with yellow pollen dust on the insides. He traces the path to a grave whose epitaph in Urdu reads:

Shaheed Mushtaq Ahmad Najar

Muhammad Sultan was a talented carpenter before he fell from a roof while working and permanently injured his left arm. And just when the injured arm had begun to heal he, against the doctor's advice, went back to work again. The internal soft-tissue injury worsened to a haematoma. After a failed surgery, his arm was declared unfit for carpentry or any manual work.

He was a master of *khatamband*, a lattice designer. Before cutting wood for use, he would smell it to gauge its quality. He specialized in mixing the classical and the modern styles, producing something that both old and young Kashmiris liked. No one in the entire village could rival his truss work. He was an expert on doors and windows—the thick part of work in carpentry. With each drag on the hookah, he came up with a new idea.

Carpentry was not only work or a source of livelihood for him, but an art form too. Art through which he expressed himself. Once at work, he would passionately sink into it. Sometimes he worked through the night. He would even work on Fridays, against custom, when all the carpenters and masons took the day off. He never actually cared for money until it really began to bother him. He was more of a dissolute artist than a time-bound carpenter. 'His hands are worth their weight in gold,' that is what almost all his customers would say after marvelling at his work. It was because of his talent that people tolerated his truancies and wild habits.

But Sultan had a shortcoming too: he was not a diligent worker. He took projects on a whim. He would hardly ever take partners or apprentices. He liked to work alone. Sometimes he would disappear for days, and later compensate for his absence by working overtime. His second romance, after carpentry, was accompanying the local militants around the village. He'd help them with anything, fetch them cigarettes and lavish money on them.

The situation with his arm depressed him. It became impossible to work, to hold tools in his left hand. Then he started taking projects on a contract basis, employing other carpenters and directing them. But their designs and work neither impressed nor satisfied his customers. Though his employees took all his directions, they never really followed them to the letter. They even cheated him of his share of the commission. Eventually, his financial situation deteriorated.

His fate grew worse—his eldest daughter was returned by her in-laws for the sixth time in four years of marriage, for not fulfilling the demands of dowry. The last time she had returned with a swollen wrist and her sniveling, sick, one-year-old baby girl. Her husband, the driver of a bus, had wrung her wrist in an argument and thrown her out of his house. But at her father's house, the eldest daughter behaved as though she was just on a visit. She even waffled to her sisters about her in-laws, praising them as if they were good people and as though nothing had happened. She talked about the 'generosity' of her in-laws' neighbours. She described her brother-in-law, his tastes in food. These details bored and irritated her sisters.

Sultan was struggling with his two other daughters at home. His middle daughter was in her late thirties, a spinster, a nearly illiterate girl, who, after her father's injury, had been supporting the household with her skills at needlework. She worked well into the night, tortured her eyes, strained and overburdened herself and gained weight and premature wrinkles on her face. She was the most beautiful among her sisters, but there was an unattended fuzz of hair over her upper lip that made her look ugly now. Lately, she had been running short of work and had taken to secretly begging at the shrine of Makhdoom Sahib on Fridays. She would slip on a long, dirty, black burka and leave home saying that she was visiting the shrine to pray to God. But Muhammad Sultan had begun to suspect that her veiled expeditions were for another reason altogether—that she was out hustling to earn some money. He was furious but tried not to show it, especially as he never wanted to follow her to confirm his suspicions.

His youngest daughter had left school at the secondary level when Sultan's wife died of a colon haemorrhage. Since her mother's death, she had looked after the whole household. Her presence in the house was a very quiet one; sometimes her own father couldn't feel her around. She almost didn't exist for him. She was just like the family cow she fed, washed, milked and cleaned. Whenever she cried, she didn't make a sound, just leaked tears which quietly streamed down her cheeks like melting pearls. She had been born just before Mushtaq, Muhammad Sultan's only son, who died in his adolescence.

Mushtaq had distanced himself from school and books and instead followed a group of local militants like his father had. One day, Mushtaq stayed behind with an armed group in a hideout—a posh house in Nishat. In the middle of the night, the hideout was raided and he was the only one who could not escape. He was killed in the kitchen.

The next morning, Muhammad Sultan managed to go to the house and see his dead son. After looking at the bullet-riddled body lying face down on the kitchen floor, he fainted. When he regained consciousness, he found that Mushtaq was being placed on a bier. The funeral was attended by the militants. Wearing masks, they merged with the funeral procession and later directed the graveyard management committee to get a quality memorial headstone chiselled for their friend. They wanted to have the headstone inscribed with an Urdu epitaph, with the title *Shaheed* before the boy's full name, which would signify that he had died for the cause of Kashmir's freedom. 'The outfit will be proud to bear all the expenses', the area commander had assured the graveyard management committee.

A few days after the burial, a shiny black granite tombstone was erected at the grave with a beautifully calligraphed Urdu epitaph in sparkling golden paint.

It was some months after his son's death that Muhammad Sultan suffered the accident in which he damaged his left arm. Soon after the accident, his elder daughter was returned and the middle one lost her work. All possible sources of income disappeared. Vexed, he berated himself between sips of endless cups of salty *nuun* tea and puffs from filterless cigarettes.

He had often heard people mention how Sataar Wagay, one of his neighbours, whose son the Army had tortured to death and dumped in the river, managed to get an ex gratia compensation of one lakh rupees sanctioned by the government. In the beginning, when not burdened by his own tragedies, Muhammad Sultan hated Sataar Wagay for accepting compensation. He even called him a traitor for selling his son's sacrifice to the government. But then Muhammad Sultan became confused when Rahman Parray, another neighbour, who had even been an active member of a separatist organization, distorted the facts surrounding his younger brother's killing by the Army and accepted compensation of one lakh rupees.

Who was right, Wagay or Parray, or himself? Baffled, Muhammad Sultan remained indecisive until his own conditions forced him to think about applying for compensation. Initially he hated himself for even thinking about asking the government for money. He wrestled with himself day and night.

He was already heavily in debt. Every morning the local grocer would come to the house and threaten to take away Sultan's cow to settle his account. He even owed the neighbourhood baker and barber. He had stopped passing their shops and now took longer routes, back and side paths, whenever he had to leave the village. But when his baby granddaughter was diagnosed with acute pneumonia, he gave up. Finally, he threw off the guise of commitment to the cause of freedom, ignored his guilt, and applied for compensation. He tried as much as possible to hide this from Gul Baghwaan, one of his close childhood friends, who had vehemently rejected an offer of compensation after his son was killed in a firing incident.

Now, the only hurdle that came between Muhammad Sultan and his compensation was the word *Shaheed*, conspicuously engraved on his son's gravestone. If discovered, the word could ruin his chances of compensation.

※

The graveyard is a plateau studded with stones and clumps of hemp and irises. It is away from the village houses and nestled on the edge of a vast expanse of paddy fields. As Muhammad Sultan sees the irises in the cloud-dimmed evening, the first stray thought that crosses his mind is how much better it would be to replace the cacti at his home with irises.

He waits for the darkness to grow thicker. He stands beside the grave of his son, folded his hands on his chest and begins to mumble *fateha*, prayer for the dead. With the growing darkness of the dusk comes a drizzle. Soon the voice of the muezzin from a nearby mosque floats into the air and mingles with the hissing rain. The wet mud sticks to the soles of his shoes, exposing patches of ochre under the upper layer of earth.

A few minutes later, when the rain stops, he holds the blunt chisel with his trembling left hand against the word *Shaheed*. He repeatedly strikes. The sounds of metal clanking and the hammer's whumping travel through the earth and reach down to Mushtaq Ahmad Najar. On one strike the pointed end of the chisel slips, misses the mark and scrapes off the name *Mushtaq* instead.

The Ex-militant

It had long been true, and prisoners knew this better than anyone, that the poorer you were the more likely you were to end up in jail. This was not just because the poor committed more crimes. In fact, they did. The rich did not have to commit crimes to get what they wanted; the laws were on their side. But when the rich did commit crimes, they often were not prosecuted, and if they were they could get out on bail, hire clever lawyers, get better treatment from judges. Somehow, the jails ended up full of poor black people.

—Howard Zinn, *A People's History of the United States*

Only yesterday I was no different than them, yet I was saved. I am explaining to you the way of life of a people who say every sort of wicked thing about me because I sacrificed their friendship to gain my own soul. I left the dark paths of their duplicity and turned my eyes toward the light where there is salvation, truth, and justice. They have exiled me now from their society, yet I am content. Mankind only exiles the one whose large spirit rebels against injustice and tyranny. He

*who does not prefer exile to servility is not free in
the true and necessary sense of freedom.*
                                        —Khalil Gibran

*L*et's begin; but first let's make sure that you aren't
disturbed by this surprise interview.

Izhar sahab, you are asking me if you disturbed me.
You or people like you cannot disturb me. And especially
when you say you are doing a story on ex-militants. I
must confess, you are not like most of my neighbours
who despise me. You are not like the government officials
who go inquiring about me in the neighbourhood, then
come to me with skeptical eyes and creased brows. You
are not like Aslam, the one from the power department,
who is yet to be sure whether or not he should give me
a permanent electricity connection. And you certainly
are not like Nazir of the water department or like the
authorities from gas or ration or revenue, or even like
the members of the Mohalla committee here.

Stigma. Every month I have to show up in the Raj
Bagh police station. Earlier it was every week. It is
impossible to get registered for certain important things
now. Passport and all other big registrations could only
be had in dreams. Even TV cable operators are inquisitive
about me.

But you are different. Not only because we have
known each other for some time now—from the day
we had a long conversation in my autorickshaw while
I was taking you to Lal Chowk—but because you are a

writer. And so, you still have that human element alive inside you.

❦

Continue. I won't cut the thread.

Why you want to write my story, I don't know. But it is interesting, in the first place, to note that you are going to write about an inconspicuous person like me; however, useless I may seem to myself now.

First of all, please put that notepad aside and take that cup to your lips; the tea is already getting cold. Yes, I know you hesitate because you look at my daughter Insha with such worry and mercy.

What happened to her?

Don't worry. She will be all right as soon as our *Truis* Peer, the local chemist, comes with some injections for fast relief … It is just a small cup of tea. Please don't hesitate.

Three days have passed and yet Insha's fever is adamant. *Truis* Peer promised to come and check on her, but hasn't. Twice I paced up and down to his shop but … If he doesn't heed the emergency I'll pull my autorickshaw up and rush her to the hospital.

Infection? I don't understand what the root cause of her fever is—maybe I don't want to know. But my immediate concern is the fever itself. She is stable, but the fever must go.

Stress. Maybe Insha is missing her old school and doesn't like the government school. But harbouring this doubt only wrenches me from within. It reminds me of my helplessness ...

Destiny. It's actually my own fault, or perhaps that of my stars. I don't know. I couldn't have afforded a patch of land in a better place, not after our joint family split and scattered around old Raj Bagh. But maybe I could have chosen Mehjoor Nagar instead. It's noisy, over-populated, cheaper, forlorn and threatened by occasional floods, but it is still better than this place.

Since it's on the riverbank, it's bad here in summer. The public utility lands, where I once played football and later practised with my Kalashnikov, have been usurped by construction mafia. Everything old and beautiful is slowly vanishing. Local land brokers sold plots to migrants from places like Haft Chinar, Fateh Kadal, Karfali Mohalla, Baba Dam, Barbarshah, Shaheed Gunj and as far as Tral and Pulwama. All those who couldn't expand in the congested downtown of Srinagar are buying the land at cheaper rates here. The brokers even threw attractive baits to the revenue officials and got an abysmal, metre-wide sewage canal dug around the one-roomed shanties of the area, such as mine. The canal comes to an end at my small house and yawns at it. I have barely tackled the diverse neighbours and the way they throw their garbage into the drain. I hardly find eggshells, orange rind, chicken entrails, bloodied cotton, insulin syringes or discarded condoms here, as I do at Hyderpora or Nishat or at posh Raj Bagh, when I drop passengers at these places ... please don't look at me with those intrigued eyes. I do observe these things whenever I come across garbage dumps in certain places. My ridiculous habit, if that's what you want to call it.

*

How do you manage here?

We have adjusted our olfactory senses to the stink of the overflowing sewage. But it becomes unbearably difficult in the evening when mosquitoes begin to throng the gutter. I stick strips of newspaper over the windows to keep these bloodsucking creatures away. After Insha fell sick, I hung a net around her bedding, stuffed its hem under her mattress. Yet in the middle of the night, a bumbling gnat still managed to feast on her toe and leave her sleepless, restless. I sweep off stiff, dry, upturned carcasses of them into a plastic dustpan, studying their banded thoraxes.

More than the open garbage piles, the main attraction for the mosquitoes is the wild daisy that has spread all over the place. It offers them daytime shelter and also covers the pools of gutter spillage.

*

There is still no sign of Peer's arrival. Her forehead feels warmer. If Peer doesn't arrive in the next ten minutes I must rush my girl to the hospital. And then you'll have to bear with me. I understand. Either Peer is busy at this late hour with the regular hypertension patients or he must be engaged in gossip with some ill housewives. He might be at the village school where he teaches, or he might be at the shrine of Dastageer Sahib at Khanyar, checking on his accounts. He is one of the shareholders of the daily *nazraana*, the propitiation people pay for their sins. But I hope he does not nag me for having made my girl 'a spectacle for three days and done nothing'. First of all he'd call me by my caste, not by my name. Then he would tell me, in front of his patients, 'What are you waiting for? You want her to die? Go and admit her into the hospital. Rush!' And then he would glance around at his patients, expect an approving look from them.

'Ghulam Mohiuddeen! Don't wait for me to return. If you want to go out, lock the main door and keep the key under the shoe!' my wife hollers from the kitchen. Did you hear that? Of course you did. You cannot hide that smirk. The water flowing from the tap, the plop of the drip, the clanging of plates, pots and spoons, the hissing of the pressure cooker—everything has abruptly stopped, signalling her departure. It is her time to go around in the neighbourhood, pay a visit to the sick or just confirm the neighbours' well-being.

Ghulam Mohiuddeen! I hate my name. I become angry with my late father for giving me an elderly name such as this. Why on earth couldn't he think of a younger-sounding one? Maybe Fayaz, like Fayaz Shah, my companion from the outfit I had worked for. He was older than me by years, but younger in name.

Even Fayaz's father, an engineer, had a name that sounded young: Farooq. Right from the start, Fayaz has been a question mark, a sickle, hovering over my head.

He holds an important position in the story I'm going to tell you.

*

Can you tell me how it all began?

The '90s were a very frenetic time. You know all of it but let me summarise it again to connect it to what I want to tell you. Thousands of Kashmiris had begun marching on every street, road and bazaar in endless processions. Men, women, children, old, young—everyone. Everyone chanted the same slogan:

> *Hum kya chahtay?*
> *Azaadi!*
> (What do we want?
> Freedom!)

There were vowing green headbands on almost every forehead. The flags people waved, the placards they flailed—all had the same message: Freedom. Elderly women would kiss the brows of the boys leaving their homes to cross the mountains into Pakistan. Toffees and petals were showered on them, something that happens to bridegrooms leaving to meet their brides.

Back home, militants would strut around like soldiers, with Kalashnikovs slung across their shoulders, wearing multi-pocket ammunition jackets. I was so stung with passion that I too would imagine myself walking like that, and being seen walking like that.

Then?

We crossed the border together, Fayaz Shah who belonged to my neighbourhood, Irshad Beigh from the Srinagar Downtown, and I. We were trained in one camp, returned together and brandished similar guns. I was promoted to the position of area commander. I was the boss, but it was always Fayaz Shah who gave the orders.

Still, I never compared myself to him. Not until the day we first went into action, in Lal Chowk.

During the ambush, Fayaz was to be my cover and wait for my signal, but when Irshad signalled the cue, it was Fayaz who opened fire, not me, not even Irshad. I couldn't even cock my gun. My shivering finger touched the trigger several times, but I couldn't bring myself to pull it. I felt weak in the knees. My bowels rumbled and I felt a dire urgency to sprint to the toilet. *I can't fire.* I was too ashamed to admit this, even to myself. The sound of gunfire sounded from all around me. I realized I had crawled on my belly to a point where I had become a cover for Fayaz and Irshad. So Fayaz had become the boss.

I peeked over the wall I was hiding behind. The only thing I could see were cartridges falling from Fayaz's smoking AK-47. I lost sight of Irshad.

Fayaz was very happy that day. He had gunned down two troopers and kept telling me, 'You kill for the first time, and then the rest becomes easy.'

Overnight, Fayaz became a hero in the area. He got a Mithun Chakraborty hairdo and assumed Sanjay

Dutt's prance, as was the rage in those days. He began to court a local elder's younger daughter who had earlier thwarted every attempt he had made to woo her. As for me, my shivering fit refused to go for days. I accepted that I was either a coward or Allah only knows what. I could never kill.

Continue.

In early 1991, we had an assignment from the outfit to stencil slogans of the freedom struggle on the walls in Raj Bagh. Fayaz, Irshad and I were partners again, daubing the walls of the locality with green paint. Fayaz left his share of work to me and Irshad. He didn't like this painting business, he said, but only pulling triggers. He sat beside me and smoked a cigarette. We were talking about our mission when an Army patrol caught us unawares.

Just a second. Side A is full. Let me turn the cassette ... Continue.

We were blindfolded and loaded into the back of a one-tonne Army truck. The men who had captured us kicked and abused us the whole way.

When our blindfolds were finally removed, we found ourselves in a musty, windowless room. There was a lone bulb that glowed softly. I sensed later that there was a coarse black blanket under us.

The following days were spent in torture and fear. I often fainted in front of the men with handlebar moustaches on their inscrutable faces. They came in turns carrying registers. They interrogated us, extracting right, affirmative answers to wrong, twisted questions. They would note down, leave and then come back. They were impervious to our responses and screams. They would just roll a cement roller on your legs, let suspended burning tyres drip on your bare back, pour buckets of dirty water over you and rattle you with electricity until you'd puke out some broken pieces of vague information. In the moments of partial consciousness, Sakeena's face would dart before my eyes. Or I would remember my mother, doing the namaaz on a faded prayer rug; my father, his shaking fingers threading a needle. I saw myself trying to take shelter under an awning during a sudden rainstorm, and finally everything fading away.

I hated Fayaz when I heard about the recovery of an hour-long videotape from him. In this video, he demonstrated the use of various kinds of guns and weapons. Unlike other militants in such videos, Fayaz had chosen to show his face to the camera.

With the knitting pin worked into my organ, I broke quicker than Fayaz and Irshad. I brought a raid to my home, got my brothers beaten and got our verdant kitchen garden and the entire floor of our cowshed dug up to unveil my beloved Kalashnikov, my Chinese pistol, a fraying pouch full of bright bronze rounds, four hand grenades and a diary that maintained an account of my unit's movements.

And then?

After four weeks of torture, we were taken out into daylight and mingled with other inmates in the lawns of Papa 2, the main interrogation centre in Srinagar. I met some guards who were good to us. They would facilitate our *mulaqaat*, meeting with parents and relatives.

As more captives filed in, and as boys piled up, older detainees were shifted to other jails to make room for the new. Fayaz and I landed in Kot Bhalwal in Jammu, three hundred and something kilometres from Srinagar. Irshad was separated from us and shifted to some other place we wouldn't ever know. The non-Kashmiri inmates, those who were charged with rapes, murders and forgery, abused us in Kot Bhalwal. They called us terrorists and traitors. The food served to us was what you would throw out back home. But still, compared to the long torturous days of Papa 2, Kot Bhalwal was a heaven. I loved the daylight that streamed in through the windows of my cell. I would marvel at the dust particles dancing in the shafts of light. I learned to listen to and love the birdsong that reached through those windows.

I had never prayed regularly, but since I had nothing to do there, I began to pray five times a day. I let my beard grow and trimmed my moustaches.

Every month I saw new entries from Kashmir. Boys who had never been able to read or recite from the Quran—I taught them. Gradually, I initiated organized prayers and regular classes on the Quran. But Fayaz had begun to avoid me. Our cells were right next to each other, but I would hardly see him. His parents paid frequent visits to Kot Bhalwal. He wouldn't appear at the meals counter, would hardly be seen in the bathrooms, wouldn't come to the prayer hall. Later, a Kashmiri inmate told me about Fayaz's release. I was both happy and surprised. Fayaz's father had been bringing pashmina shawls and Burzali almonds for the entire jail staff.

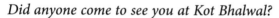

Did anyone come to see you at Kot Bhalwal?

It took my father and mother at least six months to reach me. They had never stepped out of the Banihal mountains before, but managed to make it all the way to sweltering Kot Bhalwal, carrying dry-cleaned Khansuits, toothpaste, toothbrushes, combs, bars of soap, cakes of detergent, sweaters, jackets, undergarments, hooded shoes, a pair of nylon slippers, fresh oranges, a packet of mixed dry fruit and a wrist watch. They brought a radio set too, but weren't permitted to carry it into the jail.

There was talk, tears, smiles, sighs, benedictions and news from home—killings, disappearances, crackdowns, curfews, our cow's giving birth to a heifer. Everyone was going to celebrate it with cheese made from the thick, first post-delivery milk of the mother cow. Then there was the sad news: my eldest brother's wife had given birth to a second daughter.

There was mention of the newly built bunkers and

details of political killings. They gave me an account of elimination of some innocent persons on mere suspicion, the killing of my first cousin Muhammad Yousuf Dar of Daddgam, the loss of my group mates, the death of my successor, Area Commander Shakeel Ganie, Cover Commander Javaid Dar and Aijaz and Bilal and Ishfaq and ... a whole lot of them. The conversation even touched Wali Mot, a widely known slavering lunatic, who was pitted with bullets for having lobbed his *naar-e-kaanger*, a portable brazier with hot embers, over a trooper in the crackdown. Nobody had been allowed to touch his bleeding body till he bled to death. I offered in-absentia funeral prayers, for all the lost souls, in the jail, and would later also visit the graves in person and offer *fateha* and dust the weather-beaten epitaphs to properly read the dates.

Also, there was a slight mention of Sakeena. She was still waiting for me, having rejected the formal marriage proposal of a local plumber.

Oh! Achha!

I asked my father about Fayaz. I was told that his father had flown him to Bangalore to study engineering.

What happened to Irshad finally? Did you ever hear from or about him?

After my release, I saw Irshad in the newspapers, but I could never meet him in person. He had joined Hurriyat by then and had married a lady doctor. Irshad came

from a well to do Beigh family. Besides other assets, he
had inherited one hundred and seventeen acres of apple
orchards. He had become an active separatist leader,
enjoying Indian security and local respect. He had begun
donning waist-coats to look charismatic. For a man like
me, he had become inaccessible.

✦

Three long years of my life were lost in Kot Bhalwal.

A fortnight after my release in 1993, my father lost
his battle with esophageal cancer. Then my mother
followed him a year later, but not before she supported
me in my efforts to marry Sakeena. It was difficult for
ex-militants to find wives and Sakeena's parents were
against our marriage. So my mother helped us with our
court marriage.

A month after my mother's death, our joint family
split into a cluster of nuclear families. My elder brothers
distributed our family land in old Raj Bagh, the cattle
and the copperware, amongst the siblings. Our ancestral
home was sold to a shawl merchant from downtown
Srinagar and the cash divided unevenly.

I got some copperware, and a residual patch of
land that I sold, thank Allah, and the money almost
sufficed to construct this one-roomed house and buy
a secondhand, old-model autorickshaw. My brothers
cut off a considerable amount from the share of cash I
was to receive. 'Father spent bundles of currency on the
journeys he took to visit you in Kot Bhalwal,' they said. It

was futile to argue with them. To tell them that even they knew it so well that father had visited me only once in Kot Bhalwal and that wouldn't have cost much. But they simply wouldn't accept.

Construction of this shanty seemed nearly impossible in the beginning, but, thank God, I managed to get it built. The entire wood used in the walls had to be bought on credit. It took me four years to repay the account at the hardware store. Not literally, I, actually for one, worked as a labourer for my house, with the other labourers, even though my back had long given up. I would tie a lumbar belt in the morning and untie it in the evening; I'd carry bags loaded with wood, I'd roll stones for the tin roof, would sit with a claw hammer in my hand and straighten bent rusty nails for hours in the evenings to make them fit for reuse.

*

What was the social response to your release?

It took me nearly two years to grow accustomed to the estranged neighbourhood. Many things had changed. New things had happened and many old things had vanished. New realities had to be accepted, like the obscenely opulent hotels that had sprung up in the swathes of land that had once been orchards.

I am going to share with you something very, very personal because I trust you.

Please.

In the first year of my marriage, I was nervous about

having children. In Papa 2, they had squeezed my organ and tried to crush my balls. I wasn't sure about my capabilities to father children. The coming of my daughter proved that my worry was unnecessary.

*

Continue.

Life had somehow again begun to assume some meaning with my marriage and subsequently with Insha's birth. A year passed, then another. One night we woke up to a loud thumping on the main door. I was terrified. I could feel losing some drops of pee.

I answered the door to find a posse of plainclothesmen.

I was bundled into a numberless white Sumo, Insha crying and screaming in my wake.

Again?

Yes. This time I was not blindfolded but driven around in such a convoluted manner that I couldn't keep track of where I was being taken. The men didn't speak. Once again, I was tortured for three days, handed over to ruthless men who inflicted the same treatment on me as all those years ago at Papa 2. It's hard to narrate difficult things over and over again.

Indeed it is.

Even you cannot repeat them in your story. So many miserable things in a story make it stale for readers and listeners. People wouldn't like to publish such stuff. They have to take care of the market, the target buyer. I understand. You can trim the narrative according to your own judgment, I won't mind. But do change the names, please.

Anyway, where was I? Sorry, I keep having these memory lapses. Please remind me what I was saying …

The second time you were picked up …

This time I had a clear understanding of what it was all for. It was a lesson to be learnt and digested quietly: that I wasn't ever supposed to resume my earlier life. The detention and torture was a threat, a warning …

Would you like one more cup of tea? Please have one more. See, you haven't touched the biscuits. At least have some snacks from that bowl. Please scoop out a spoon for my sake …

Three days later, I was handed over to the Raj Bagh police. After some paperwork, I was released and sent home, pale and limping. I resumed driving my autorickshaw and behaved as if nothing had occurred. As if I had been somewhere, visiting my in-laws, perhaps. Now, Sakeena looked ever more worried about me than she had before.

What do you think about Kashmir? About the situation here?

Confused. I can't talk about that at all. I can talk about anything on earth, but not about the future of Kashmir. Its present is so confused already.

I can only say that things have become worse. Almost all the things—familial, social, financial, political, and so on. We are stuck.

Recently I was called by the principal of Insha's

school. I was informed that she was going to be expelled.
The reason was my failure to pay her tuition fees for the
last four months in a row.

❦

*Just a second. Side B is full. Let me change the cassette ...
Continue.*

Fayaz Shah returned from Bangalore without any
degree in engineering. He, like many ex-militants, slid
into mainstream politics. When I was on my way to meet
the principal of my daughter's school, I saw Fayaz. He
looked clean in his white Khansuit and jet black waist-
coat, supervising men who were tying buntings of Janta
Party all over the place.

It had become difficult and awkward for me to meet
him and remind him of the old days.

My life began to feel jinxed. Every bad thing was
happening to me. I wasn't able to deposit the fees at my
daughter's school. My autorickshaw devoured a major
chunk of my earnings. Every now and then, one or
the other part of its engine would flop. One scorching
afternoon, the clutch cable snapped midway while I was
carrying a passenger to the Bone and Joint Hospital.
Two days later, the vehicle started producing explosive
sounds, which the local mechanic diagnosed as resulting
from a block in the carburettor. But more than anything,
my biggest worry was Insha's education. I went to her
school again to ask for more time to deposit her fees.

'Look, only the trustees can help in this case. I have no objection if they allow you some time or even waive the entire dues,' said the principal.

For some time I stared at the sky blue globe on his table. Finally, I asked him, 'Could you please tell me who among the trustees I must approach to make my request in this regard? I don't know any trustee.'

'Of course. The chief trustee is Mr. Fayaz Shah. You may meet him.'

[Sigh.]

Psychosis

*Look at how many children you can have. Now
you are going to have our children.*
—Robert Fisk, *The Rapes Went on Day and
Night, The Independent,* Feb 8, 1993

Rape is always torture.
—Manfred Nowak, Special Rapporteur,
United Nations

Each receding paranoid trooper diminishes, shrivels
and fades in the convex mirror of the 407 bus,
dragging behind itself a long ribbon of the road. The
road bends at Dalgate and stretches through the
downtown of Srinagar. Sakeena is one of the thirty
seated, standing, lurking, hanging, tired, baffled, happy,
inscrutable, serious or garrulous passengers who cram
the bus, pushing and nudging each other in the aisle.
She makes it a point to spot each and every passing
autorickshaw in the reflection of the side view mirror,
read its registration number and especially scan the
fashionable petty romantic Urdu couplet stencilled on
its back. It is a habit she has nurtured over the years.

Sakeena shares half a grubby seat with an elderly fat
lady. The lady has squeezed her so much that Sakeena feels

breathless. A young woman stands in the overcrowded aisle, holding onto the roof handrail, stealing glances at Sakeena. Sakeena doesn't care about the young woman's staring at the careless way she conducts herself. That when Sakeena's dupatta slips down her head, falls off her shoulder and begins to sweep the floor of the bus, she doesn't care to lift it up. The young woman studies Sakeena's raw beauty: her fair skin and sharp features—a straight, sleek, long nose, almond-shaped eyes under perfectly arched brows with the extra hair she has long given up tweezing. The woman stares at the plump contours of Sakeena's cheeks and notices the prominent ugly oily pores on her nose.

Sakeena's elder child, ten-year-old daughter Insha, has hennaed ducks on both of Sakeena's palms. Her fingers are fair, her nails gnarled at their tips. Her sun-kissed hair is slightly dusty and loose over her temples. Although she has deprived herself of all jewellery and make-up, she still wears silver anklets. And a little silver stud glints in her right nostril. But her nose is a bit runny, causing her to occasionally snivel. A black thread with a rectangular amulet is her most prominent adornment.

A flat plastic bag sits on her lap. Before she alights at Rainawari Chowk, she fumbles for her medical prescriptions and reports, reassuring herself that she has carried them along. She is on her way to the Government Psychiatric Diseases' Hospital, the only one of its kind in the valley of Kashmir. She has been visiting it for the last six years.

When she disembarks, her silver anklets jingle, commanding the attention of other passengers.

❦

Today there are more patients than usual, jostling at the sparsely barred window which doubles as a reception counter of the Out Patient Department. She has to struggle to queue up behind a morose old woman—whose son, Sakeena learnt, has been killed in front of her eyes—and pass her consultation card to the assistant behind the window and collect the token for her turn.

Clusters of uniformed nurses return from the canteen after their noon tea, chatting and lightly chuckling. Some security guards are helping push an old man's wheelchair up the cemented entrance ramp. The old man had stopped feeling his legs after an Army tanker ran over his only son. A woman, who pushes the wheelchair of the old man, waves a wet X-ray film of a skull in the air, drying it up. For some days now the paraplegic man has been butting walls. The neuropsychiatric consultant wanted a radiograph of the old man's head. If it is confirmed that the man has hurt his skull, because he has also stopped speaking, it might lead to further investigations.

The white ambulance stands quietly in a section of the hospital compound shaded by a wall, uncertainly sleeping through its moments of peace for some indefinite time, its melted front tyres tilted right. The two old chinars behind the old barrack-like hospital building are completely leafless, the snow-crowned top of mount

Harmukh behind them looms close in the view against a cerulean November sky.

Sakeena's turn to enter Dr. Imtiyaz's consultation chamber is just after a young man with frissons. She has been noticing him and his seizures for all the six years now. The man is accompanied by an elderly woman. He has been silent and shaking from the day he forgot to lower down a waterboarded captive who had been suspended upside down in a police torture cell. That is what the elderly lady, who happens to be his mother, is narrating to everyone. The young man was a constable in the State Task Force—a special police wing in Kashmir constituted by the government to eliminate the militants—and had been on duty, watching over a dangling upside-down captive through one night, and had fallen asleep before he could loosen the captive's rope and put him back on the ground. When he had woken up later, the captive was already dead.

❀

Dr. Imtiyaz is glad about the improvement Sakeena has made over a long period of time. He crosses out the drugs he had earlier prescribed for her query seizures, but she has to continue taking Olanzapine 20 mg BD, twice a day, for her cycloid psychosis.

Six years ago when she was admitted to this hospital for *acute onset of confusion, delusions, hallucinations, altered behaviour, pan anxiety, elation, happiness or ecstasy of high degree, self-blaming and mood swings—*

with her bleeding, razor-nicked wrists—she had to be literally tied to her bed in the general ward. The doctors and her attendants had been prepared for her transfer to the asylum section of the hospital, just in case. But after showing a reasonable comeback, she had stayed in the ward. And later that year, with some psychotic symptoms intact, she had birthed a baby boy, Bilal.

Considering Sakeena's condition, Dr. Imtiyaz had been kind enough to adopt Insha for that crucial year, and taken care of her like he would of his own children. His twelve years of experience treating Post Traumatic Stress Disorder (PTSD) patients had melted his heart, so much so that he had begun to sound irritatingly humane to his wife, relatives and friends. His patients visited him at home, some disturbed him at night. Besides free consultations, medicine and endless counselling, he had even started lending money and providing shelter to poor or distant patients and their attendants.

✱

'So, how do you feel now?' Dr. Imtiyaz asks.

'The nightmares have become infrequent. Now I don't see my body rolling down the riverbank. Nor does my bloody shalwaar appear. But the smell of sperm barely leaves me. Even pleasantly scented things smell dirty to me.'

'Good that the nightmares have abated. I hope the smell will go too. And what about the hallucinations?'

'Not too often.'

'Very good. And what about the other dreams?'

'Some days ago Ghulam Mohiuddeen came in my dream and said he couldn't return now and therefore I should take care of myself and Insha.'

'And did he only talk about you and Insha?'

'He didn't talk about anyone else.'

'Sure?'

'Sure.'

Silence.

'And did he say that you should remarry, or something like that, a hint?'

'No.'

'Are you convinced he is not alive, that he won't return?'

'One hundred per cent. My heart says he is not alive.'

'Then isn't it better that you remarry?'

Silence.

*

In her neighbourhood, the two idle men, whom Sakeena noticed in the morning when she was leaving for the hospital, are still sitting on the sill of the shop, sucking on their hookah and gossiping. They are talking about a notification the government has sent to the squatters, asking them to vacate the riverbank before they are hauled away. The government has decided to clear the area and make hanging parks along the bank to entice tourists.

When Rasheed, the shopkeeper, notices Sakeena, he suspends a customer in the middle of a deal and calls out to her. 'Excuse me, your favourite soap has come. I thought I should inform you,' he says to her flirtatiously.

'No thank you. I don't need it now,' she says brusquely, flouncing off.

'It comes with a scheme. You get a pencil for free,' he adds, but Sakeena doesn't respond.

The two men continue smoking and consider protesting instead of demanding rehabilitation from the government. Rasheed leans over the jars of confectionary and giggles softly and suggestively as she passes the shop. Before the two men turn their heads to look him in the eye, he resumes his conversation with the customer he had left hanging.

Back home, Insha is making tea for Sakeena. A pan is stewing on the gas stove. The tea comes to seethe soon, so Insha turns the knob of the stove and simmers it down to a low flame. The bubbling brown frothy tea throws the tea leaves to the walls of the pan. 'It took you long today,' Insha remarks to Sakeena, looking away from the brewing tea.

'Yes, jaana,' Sakeena responds, panting as she enters the one-room shanty house.

The house is built on a rostrum that sits on thick round wooden posts in a squatters' settlement near Zero Bridge. The settlement is looked over by tall hotels that have come up across the riverbank, shaded by a canopy of chinar branches. The river laps the wooden stairs that lead to the door of the shanty beside its attached wooden

privy. Recently the government has suddenly declared
the settlement as 'illegal encroachment'.

Sakeena tosses her plastic bag to the floor, sits in a
clean corner and gazes at the motionless houseboats
through the tiny window. Unlike in the hallucinations
earlier, the houseboats don't appear aflame to her now.

On the inside, the shanty is wallpapered with cheap
gift-wrapping paper: a pattern of white polka dots on a
purple background. In one of the corners is Sakeena's
kitchen. Glass jars filled with spices sit on wooden
shelves fixed to the wall. A pressure cooker lid hangs by
a rusty nail. Beneath the shelves, there is a gas stove and
a shallow steel tub for dish washing.

In another corner, there is a pile of bedding: a folded
quilt on a pair of pillows; pillows, in turn, topping a
folded mattress—all draped in a bedspread. And a neatly
folded mink blanket set over all.

To Sakeena's right is a roughly folded prayer rug on
a triangular shelf, tucked under an X-shaped, primer-
painted, small wooden rack. On the rack is a velvet-
encased Quran.

Wicker baskets and plastic bags hang from the rafters
of the ceiling.

Between the kitchen side and the bedding side, a
television rests on a low trestle table. Under the table there
is a bald, naked doll, a school satchel, unevenly stacked
textbooks, notebooks, a worn-out green eraser and a
pencil chewed on the top. These things belong to Insha.
The walls are dirtied with stray pencil work: amorphous

shapes of animals and birds, creatures and things that don't actually exist. The doodle is visible only to a sensitive eye—all the handiwork of Sakeena's son Bilal.

Insha strains the tea into three cups, keeps one for herself, gives one to Bilal and places another in front of her mother. She distributes peanut-studded biscuits as well.

Sakeena dips a biscuit into her cup and angrily watches Bilal scattering crumbs of his biscuit on the floor mat, his legs splayed out under him.

'Bastard!' she says, grimacing at him.

Insha widens her eyes at her mother and says, 'Please Mamma, don't.'

'See, he is good for nothing. He has spoiled the mat. I swept it this morning only.'

'Don't worry. I will clean it again,' Insha says.

Bilal looks at Sakeena. She glares back at him. The soggy part of the biscuit between her thumb and forefinger crumbles and falls into the tea.

Sakeena was married to Ghulam Mohiuddeen.

She had seen him for the first time at a friend's wedding. That was where everything had begun. For his militant background, her parents didn't approve of him. The couple went ahead and got married in court.

They came to live in the crammed squatters' settlement, all the shelter Ghulam Mohiuddeen could afford. Sakeena was still happy. It was bliss to live with the man she loved, however small, creaky and impermanent the place was.

Ghulam Mohiuddeen had had an adequate education, but because of his ex-militant status, he decided to strike out on his own and earn his livelihood by driving an autorickshaw. Since there were frequent curfews and shutdowns in the city that severely affected the public transport system, the autorickshaw job paid well.

Ghulam Mohiuddeen was very loving and caring and full of respect for Sakeena. He would smother her with surprises and gifts—shawls or sandals or suits or purses or bangles—every month.

Within the first seven days of their marriage, he bought her a TV set. 'I know you are fond of films and old songs,' he said, unwrapping the Styrofoam packing.

Insha was born a year after the marriage. Ghulam Mohiuddeen had wanted a daughter, and was delighted with her.

He was a diehard fan of the radio. He was a member of the Raj Bagh Autorickshaw Listeners' Club. Besides the daily BBC Urdu news, he listened to cricket commentary. He hardly missed any match played between India and Pakistan. At home he followed the TV broadcast too, but the radio kept mewling beside him, whining on fours, sixers, outs and commercials.

A few more years passed by. Ghulam Mohiuddeen and Sakeena began to plan a second child. To that end, he fixed up an appointment for Sakeena with a local gynaecologist. Sakeena awaited his arrival from the day's job.

That day at his autorickshaw stand, he had an argument with another driver: Bitt'a Shuad'a.

Bitt'a Shuad'a doubled as a renegade, a counter-insurgent, who had links with the local Army unit in Raj Bagh. The passengers from the stand were taken on a rotation basis. But Bitt'a would browbeat other autowalas and often snatch their passengers. That day, Bitt'a jumped the queue and seized another driver's passengers. Ghulam Mohiuddeen had been quietly tolerant of Bitta's attitude towards his colleagues, but on that day he lost his temper. He intervened and had a heated argument with Bitt'a that turned into a serious dispute when Ghulam Mohiuddeen beat him.

And on that evening Ghulam Mohiuddeen didn't come home at his normal time. Sakeena sat by the window and watched for him, looking at the spot on the riverbank road where, every evening, Ghulam Mohiuddeen would bump up his roaring autorickshaw and then descend the riverbank towards the shanty.

Later that night, it wasn't Ghulam Mohiuddeen in his auto who bounded up the road. There were two Army cars instead.

❧

A contingent of troops cordoned the shanty off. Some barged in. Sakeena tried to switch on the lights, but a dark hand pushed her aside. In the faint light filtering in from the street, she could see that four soldiers and a masked boy had barged into the shanty. Two more kept guard at the door. The whole neighbourhood seemed to be alert and listening.

The men threw her down to the ground and held her legs and arms. One of them stripped her of her shalwaar and stuffed it into her mouth. Insha shrieked, calling out to the neighbours for help. One trooper lifted Insha by the neck of her shirt and took her away.

The men didn't let Sakeena go for an hour. 'Your husband is with us, so take *care*,' they said while leaving.

As soon as the troops were gone, the neighbours rushed to the shanty. Sakeena was lying half naked on the floor, unconscious. A woman covered her with a blanket.

Sakeena raved for the next few days. Nobody had any clue about Ghulam Mohiuddeen. Her mental health deteriorated. Her neighbours admitted her to the Government Psychiatric Diseases' Hospital.

There was no such Army camp, no interrogation centre, no jail that Sakeena didn't knock the doors of while searching for Ghulam Mohiuddeen. But she found nothing, not even his autorickshaw. Finally, someone told her that Ghulam Mohiuddeen had been seen in Sonawari renegade camp.

The guards at the gate of the Sonawari camp demanded one lakh rupees in exchange for providing information about her husband. She promised to pay them the amount once it was ascertained that Ghulam Mohiuddin was there, in the camp. In the meantime, she began to borrow the money from shopkeepers like Rasheed and started begging for it in places unknown.

Then one day she went to Sonawari to pay a small amount of five thousand rupees as advance. But then the guards demanded that she sleep with them. Sakeena left, crying.

※

In the evening as the sun slumps behind the new tall buildings at Zero Bridge and birds flock back to their nests flying wingtip to wingtip, Sakeena, as usual, padlocks the door of the shanty from the outside and jumps in through the back window. She draws the curtains and switches on the lamps.

From the corner of her eye during her namaaz, she sees Bilal diddling with his sister's pencil. It is hard for Sakeena to fight the urge to slap him. Bastard! she says in her mind.

She has beaten him most often just because of what he symbolizes. He is the human shape of a painful memory.

Earlier, she has even tried killing him. She would leave him alone at home for hours so that he could wander in the shanty and consume something, anything, pick up the conspicuous green sachet of rat poison from the window ledge and fiddle with it, or pick up the knife that lies beside the gas stove and cut himself. Or die from the simple fear of being alone for hours.

In the posh colony of Raj Bagh, where Sakeena is a domestic worker, she would leave him outside in the lawns to let him eat mud. But he wouldn't.

Insha did and this bastard doesn't, Sakeena would think.

Bilal was not even properly breastfed, only granted the privilege temporarily at the insistence of Dr. Imtiyaz. He was the one who named the boy. Sakeena herself has barely uttered his name in the past six years.

Bilal resembles Sakeena. Large blue eyes, silky hair, plump red cheeks, straight snotty nose. He is always silent and confused in front of his mother, but happy with Insha.

Insha does everything for Bilal. She washes him, dresses him and feeds him. She protects him from his most dangerous enemy—his own mother.

After dinner Sakeena takes out a plastic box. She sorts through various strips of medicine—medicine for her backache and migraine and hypothyroidism—searching for her Olanzapine tablets.

While the kids watch TV, Sakeena looks away, and languidly stares at the framed picture near the clock on the wooden wall. In the picture she and Ghulam Mohiuddeen sit in a garden, both scowling at the sun.

Insha slips between Sakeena and Bilal on the bedding. She studies the henna on her mother's palms and says, 'I thought bus handrails had faded the ducks …'

'Dear foolish girl, how could it fade away only in a day,' Sakeena says, kissing Insha's brow.

For a few weeks now the mercury has been dipping. The change in weather has come as a relief. Tonight Sakeena may sleep in relative peace.

It rains at night now. And it gets a little cold inside the shanty. The thrum of the rain on the tin roof wakes Sakeena. She ensures that Insha is well covered, but finds that Bilal has rolled out of the quilt. She lies on her back in her place, considering the boy.

She comes out of the bedding, softly moves Insha aside and slides between the two children. She leaves Bilal in the cold, without his share of the quilt. After sometime Bilal curls up from the chill in the room. She looks at the boy, observes the slight rise and fall of his chest as he breathes, his incessant sighing, and the innocence of his face in sleep.

Then she carefully draws him close and covers him in a good deal of the warm quilt. For a moment, she feels like stroking his hair. But she withdraws her hand just as her fingers are about to touch him. 'Bilal,' she says under her breath and settles on her back. Tears stream quietly down her temples.

❋

It has rained heavily the whole night. In the morning when Sakeena leaves for work, she finds that Jhelum has risen. The lower steps of the stairs that lead to the door of the shanty have been submerged, forcing her to wade through the spate towards the bank, her children enfolded in the crooks of her arms. Insha is uniformed and has to go to school. Bilal has to go with Sakeena, to the houses where she cleans.

❋

One month has passed and Sakeena is once again in front of Dr. Imtiyaz. Not many patients are lined up outside the Out Patient Department today.

'So, how do you feel?' Dr. Imtiyaz asks.

'Better than last time.'

'Good. I am going to reduce the dosage, okay?'

'Your kindness.'

Some patients in the corridor of the hospital press their noses against the panes behind the meshed windows of Dr. Imtiyaz's chamber. But the doctor doesn't care to pay attention.

'And since you are improving, how about giving a thought to my suggestion?'

'Which suggestion, doctor sahab?'

'Marrying again?'

Silence.

'I can't.'

'Why?'

Long silence.

'I am still waiting for him.'

❀

When Sakeena comes back from the hospital, she finds a bevy of police men and a giant yellow bulldozer in the neighbourhood. All the squatters have gathered and they are protesting against the government. The bulldozer is being readied to shove the shanties off the riverbank. For some time, Sakeena stands still, silent, trying to convince herself that this is not a hallucination. Insha and Bilal stand in the doorway of the shanty, watching the chaos. Then, as protests intensify, Sakeena joins in.

Theft

*As long as she thinks of a man, nobody objects to
a woman thinking.*
> —Virginia Woolf, *Orlando*

Everyone here will tell you everything about you now. That *she is ... that she ... she ...*

But no one will say: that *she ... that she ... that she ...*

Shut that door. The din of the traffic is drowning your voice, and you will tell somebody something. Is it your fault that you are what you are?

First of all, say this: when you are flirted with and no one knows, you are everything; everything: a confidant, sincere, serene; and when somebody's wife comes to know about it all, about the *casual affair*, you suddenly turn out to be a thief! You suddenly become wicked, a slut, a whore, cheap, smut, whatever.

'I am going to call the police'—that is what somebody is saying now.

'Does somebody see any wrinkle of fear on my face'— is what you say in response, confidently. 'So go ahead'— is what you add under your breath, even if the girls are glaring at you.

Somebody attends to Israel and Gaza the whole day

on that little TV, but is so indifferent to the small things at home. Funny.

Who was near the cash drawer when somebody left to watch the ruckus taking place outside?

You wish you could say that it is the one who usually pilfers the out-of-demand blushers, lipsticks, nail paints, mascaras, pencils and perfumes. It is a hint. And you don't even need to give a hint.

These salesgirls, your colleagues, suddenly become honest and clean and privy to *everything* you did.

You could also have had boyfriends like them. Could have spent so much stolen money on your long cellphone-heating nightly chats. And you could have lied and said that you spent it on other things.

You sit here, suspended, heart-wrenched—perhaps waiting for the police to come—scanning the shelves full of clothes and cosmetics you would once proffer to customers. You stare out at the sun-warmed busy Residency Road through the thick glass door.

You would always wish that one day you too would be like some of the customers you attend to. Buy cosmetics for yourself and sweaters for your husband and children. Or take some time off for yourself and enjoy a relaxed stroll through Lal Chowk. Bargain with the old fisherwoman on Amira Bridge for a kilo or two of carp minnows. Peer at the Jhelum flowing under the bridge. Follow the sweating old man who struggles to push his loaded cart up the hump of the bridge. And later wonder that who this old man was? And what made him look more alone than you? Yet more inscrutable than you. You want to wonder about the man who waves those advertisement bills for government jobs, wonder if there is any chance for people like you. For the girl whose father was an ex-militant, whose prematurely aging mother has got *this and that* about herself, whose *brother* is *this and that*. You must know you don't stand a chance. As if it were your fault to be what you are.

How useless is it to remind somebody of your favours! You were asked to wash somebody's dirty tumblers, you didn't refuse. Your salary was curtailed just because you weren't keeping well for a day or two, you didn't complain. You were delegated to peddling the out-of-demand items: expired cosmetics and defective designer jewellery, at cheap rates, you didn't point out that it wasn't part of your contract. You were even asked to fetch cigarettes from that paanwala across the road and bear his teasing, which you ignored. You went around, into the huddle of onlookers, knots of gossiping government employees in the teastalls, among the cynical staff of private schools; you went promoting, selling the out-moded merchandise, and you didn't return without success. You were made to roam among pirated disc-sellers, lottery ticket vendors, ragpickers, traffic police and bunkers, and you didn't mention it. And here you are now. A *thief*!

Now you wish you died the day you were born. Or the day you were thrown out of school. Or the day your father vanished. Or the day your mother was raped. Or the day your house was dismantled on the riverside.

Stop fiddling with those broken pieces of toothpick. Move that mannequin aside. Can anybody see the Station House Officer of the police station through the glass showcase? Can somebody see him extorting his regular share from the footpath vendors and cart pushers? Yes, everybody can. He is a call away, the SHO. Now, if somebody really thinks you've stolen the money, he can be called inside. But you swear you will stay right here; you won't move an inch till the police arrive.

You won't trouble anyone any more. Here, somebody should take the key of the testers' showcase. And tell Rubeena not to look on those shelves for the shampoo. Customers don't like clueless salespersons. All shampoos are in the shampoo section.

You can't stand the insult. The sun is dwindling. Your mother will be waiting on the main road by now. She'll worry. Leave for now. If somebody still suspects you of committing the theft, your address is recorded here:

Insha Mohiuddeen
D/o Late/Missing Mr. Ghulam Mohiuddeen
Tengpora Bypass
Batamaloo, Srinagar

A Photo with Barack Obama

I am a bastard, too. I love bastards! I am bastard begot, bastard instructed, bastard in mind, bastard in valour, in everything illegitimate.
—William Shakespeare, *Troilus and Cressida*

Why do I pelt stones? This thought had never crossed my mind, I just instinctively knew when I had to don the armour and start the battle ... Enough of arguments, after all I am a stone pelter I cannot win an argument with you, for you are learned men.

... and what else can I do to express my resistance against oppression.
—Imran Muhammad Gazi, *I Am a Stone Pelter, Greater Kashmir*, 13 February 2010

There are no illegitimate children, only illegitimate parents.
—Leon R. Yankwich

The first time Biul became indifferent to his social stigma was when a policeman called him *haraamzaada*, bastard, and kicked him exactly ten times in the ribs. The policeman repeated the word each time he kicked him. Then Biul was left alone, shivering in the January night on the bare, cold, chipped cement floor of a six-by-six cell in the Batamaloo police station. Flashes of the policeman's dark hairy groin, clanking of the dangling, glinting steel buckle of his police belt, with a raised steel police logo on it, crossed his mind later. Thrice that night he asked to go to the toilet and was twice refused and forced to hold it in. He was allowed to pee only after it was ascertained that his urine had darkened his pajamas. He was kicked into the dark jail loo, reeking of stale urine. Shivering, his teeth chattered as he let his bladder go.

He piddled endlessly and tried to study the unplastered, windowless toilet that was better than the one he had at his two-room house in suburban Tengpora. He had been booked under the Public Safety Act for being the youngest stone pelter of Batamaloo. The police had recovered a bag full of stones and brick nuggets from his possession. Throwing stones at police was the only vent to his frustration and the only way to give meaning to his life, he thought.

After three days of detention, he was released when Dr. Imtiyaz, the psychiatrist, intervened and brought all sorts of intercessions for his release. Biul was only thirteen then, so Dr. Imtiyaz's pleading worked.

That was all a year ago. But now, US president Barack Obama was visiting India and stone-pelting in Kashmir would invite his attention. He could just say something about the resolution of the Kashmir issue, something the Indian State didn't want to hear. And so, the police had begun to throw the leading stone pelters into, what they called, preventive custody. Biul didn't know much about who Barack Obama was and what his visit meant, but he heard so much about him, saw so much about him on TV ahead of the visit, that, like many, he too began to lionize Obama in his thoughts. The big boys of the neighbourhood discussed Obama nonstop these days. Biul listened to them, rapt.

'... America matters ...'

'Remember his first speech as the president?'

'Yes, equality for all races, religions, regions, et cetera et cetera ...'

'He promised to withdraw troops from Afghanistan and Iraq ...'

'... Extend help to solve all political conflicts ...'

'... As far as Kashmir ...?'

'"Will bring freedom and peace," he vowed ...'

'All farce. He can't do anything. He will be the same as Bush. All farce ...'

But still:

'He is a black. He understands the pain of being deprived ...'

'... America matters ...'

And after Biul heard that many believed Obama was basically a Muslim, his own faith in him increased.

To avoid unnecessary attention, Sakeena, his mother, advised him to stay indoors for some time. He stayed at home all day, praying that the police wouldn't come to take him. Each knock on the main door set his heart racing.

Sakeena had married off her only daughter, Insha, to a villager who owned considerable land and drove his own rental Sumo. To earn bread, Sakeena had begun to stitch clothes at home and sometimes worked a spinning wheel. Her customers' frequent visits began to scare Biul. He took each knock for a police raid.

Biul avoided going upstairs to feed his seven white, fan-quilled pigeons. Instead, Sakeena dismantled the roosts, shifted the rectangular coop down to the small lawn and placed it behind the pomegranate bush. This way, the house did not remain so conspicuous in their small neighbourhood.

Biul had spent most of the school year as a truant, bunking classes with his older friends. He would quietly stow the shirt he wore at home into his worn school satchel. Along the way to school, he would furtively replace his sky blue uniform shirt with this one. The days would be spent in the desolate fallows of Batamaloo's isolated pastures, watching the cows and their heifers grazing. Sometimes he would wander into the wetlands near Gangbugh where the birds landed to peck for floating insects; he even ambled in renounced orchards, neglected places where people hardly knew him. He strolled through empty paddy fields, napped in gloomy, dense poplar grooves and willow forests. Hopping frogs would emerge from the lush green turf, cross his path and then disappear in the vast fields of mustard crops, the leaves studded with beads of iridescent dew.

Around noon the sun would gradually penetrate through the dense trees and shrubbery and rosebushes, winking in the dewed blades of grass. In the hedgerow, running along a stream that quenched the thirst of the paddy flats of Gangbugh, he would break for a minute to watch the Bihari labourers weed or plough the fields, the dew-beaded gossamer threads on the anthills glittering and twinkling like fluorescent diamonds.

He would stop for a while to marvel at all this. Halt abruptly to observe the anthills and their powder-soil raisings. Pluck all the dandelion balls and blow the little feathery parachutes away. He had trained himself to eat the choky rosehips that dangled from high bramble-bush fences.

He cherished his solitary expeditions; they helped him understand himself and his existence in the world a little better. Helped him come to terms with the guilt of his being and make a bit of sense of the absurdity of his loneliness, an absurdity most difficult to express through language.

But when there were only three months to go before the final-term exams at school, he lost his textbooks. He had spent the day as usual, exploring the fields, and later fording a stream. This was where the disaster happened. His satchel slipped and fell into the stream, floated some distance away and then clung to a tough root that leaned over the bank.

He retrieved the bag. He didn't worry about the soggy books or the smudged blue ink in his sodden notebooks, the wet pages sticking together. He figured he would dry them in the sun and recover some readable text, but he became uneasy about Sakeena's reaction to the incident. Finding out that he skipped school would upset her greatly. It would be futile to explain why he did it. She had never truly understood the things he went through, being a 'bastard'—the social ostracization he faced from his classmates and the neighbourhood boys, the extra punishments he endured at school.

Ultimately, Biul decided not to hide the wet satchel from Sakeena and steeled himself for the consequences. When he came clean, a silence fell between them. After a while she surprised him by saying, 'If you don't enjoy school you shouldn't be kept from doing what interests you.'

Biul stared at her, mouth agape. 'No, I must study, ' he said seriously, making up his mind then and there to slog. Sakeena didn't say anything because she believed him. Biul fared well in the final exams.

The only person in the neighbourhood who really sympathized with Biul was Mohsin, several years older than him. Mohsin was an apprentice to his maternal uncle, the photographer and owner of Raja Photo Studio in Tengpora. Mohsin had been orphaned at age two. His parents had been swept away by an avalanche in Ramban, the mountainous track on the Srinagar-Jammu highway. They had been on their way to Jammu to consult a neurologist for his father's consistent migraine.

Mohsin had been brought up by his uncle. He had scarcely gone to school. He wasn't allowed to leave the studio or talk to the customers or socialize and mingle with the boys of the neighbourhood. He knew all about Biul, his life, and occasionally communicated with him through gestures when his uncle was not around.

Biul had already grown indifferent to the public taunting, to the grunting of the assistant Imam of the local mosque who would always try to keep him from entering the house of God, implying that illegitimate people desecrated mosques. The mosque management committee tried to keep him from touching the Quran, and the big boys overtly nudged him or pinched his thigh during the namaaz.

He had vowed to pay them back in the same coin. If they nudged him he would nudge back, come what may. If they called him *haraamuk* or *zinhuuk*, he would tell them about their mothers' and sisters' and wives' and daughters' illicit affairs and dirty scandals. He would make them wonder if he really were, in fact, the only illegitimate child in the neighbourhood.

One evening, he went straight to Raja Photo Studio, looking for Mohsin. From a distance he saw that the lights in the studio were on and the glass door shut, signalling the presence of Mohsin's uncle. He stopped, turned and scampered as far as the reed ponds near the

Tengpora-Bypass crossing. And one more time, the vivid flashes of the policeman's dark hairy groin, clanking of the dangling, glinting steel buckle of his police belt, with a raised steel police logo on it, crossed his mind. Biul tried to cry, and each time he did, no tears would come. When he was sure that no one was around, he shouted and screamed at the top of his lungs until he felt a little relieved.

That year there were violent protests across the valley of Kashmir against an incident in Shopian, with protestors accusing the Army and police of abducting, raping and murdering two women who had gone to visit their apple orchard. The news of the incident brought back old memories to Sakeena. Biul had heard all about that terrible night from various people. The news of Shopian made him even more alert to Sakeena's evident distress. He watched her chew the edge of her dupatta all day.

Amidst public outcry, youths pelted stones at the police and the Army. On the main road and Bypass crossing, masked big boys clashed with the troops dressed in riot-gear. Those who were scared of participating hid behind turnoffs in the streets and watched. Later in the evening, the big boys would call the hiders 'cowards' and 'fence-sitters'. Biul was one among them.

He had more reason to fling stones than anyone else, he knew. He felt like stoning his own slander-infested existence, the forever unknown face of that trooper, whichever of the five men it had been, who had raped his mother. Gradually, he slid into the circle of big boys and the next year, the police cameras caught him in the front ranks of stone pelters at Batamaloo. In his idle wanderings, he had perfected the technique of skipping stones thrice on the surface of a pond before drowning it. Now, in the stone battles with the police and Army, his parabolic hurl landed smack-bang on the target. He became famous in Batamaloo, and was called Shoaib Akhtar after the Pakistani fast-bowler. He earned new respect from the big boys, those who had bullied him earlier.

Before lobbing them, Biul would examine the texture and dimensions of the stones, heft them, consider their edges and roughness. Each time he threw a stone, it felt like he was shedding off a burden. He used the slingshot too. In one pelting spree, he injured three police constables in a row, like a clean-bowled hat-trick. One of his targets was a policewala whose glass shield read *Sexy Nazir*. Biul made the stone ricochet off a telegraph pole and fly into the policewala's face from under the glass face-guard of his helmet, breaking his lower jaw. All his companions noticed the art and skill in his performance, and were impressed.

That evening the big boys brought him home on their shoulders. He stood apart, reserved, unsmiling.

Strangely, the only person who did not appreciate Biul's ventures was Mohsin. This disapproval, in turn, made Biul edgy. He wanted to speak to him, but the constant presence of his uncle didn't give him any chance. His uncle was already extremely angry at the indefinite shutdowns in Batamaloo, which were affecting his business drastically. Even the routine passport photography had taken a hit, forcing Mohsin's uncle to sell phone recharges to make ends meet.

Sakeena seemed indifferent to Biul's new exploits. She did appreciate how society had begun to respect him, taking him into the fold.

One night, the police raided the homes of the known stone pelters. They dragged the big boys out and kicked them all the way to their battered white Rakshak jeeps. Biul was also plucked from his home and caught red-handed with a bagful of stones.

❧

The first thing the police did with Biul and the other captives was lash them naked with the buckle of their leather belts. Then they photographed them and opened files on them. This 'criminal' record would stick to Biul for the rest of his life:

Name: Bilal Ahmad (alias Biul alias Shoaib Akhtar)
S/o: Ghulam Mohiuddeen [sic]*
Age: 12
Designation: Student
R/o: Tengpora, Batamaloo, Srinagar.

---

* The recorded parentage is not certain. The father mentioned here has been missing since 1998. Real pedigree remains unconfirmed.

Crime: Stone pelting. Injured eleven on-duty policemen, three of them seriously (the detainee has been booked under the Jammu & Kashmir Public Safety Act 1978 for disturbing the peace of and waging war against the state).

Location of crime: Tengpora, Batamaloo, Srinagar.

Location of arrest: Tengpora, Batamaloo, Srinagar.

In their seizure memo, the police wrote:

Arms/articles recovered at the time of arrest: A white plastic bag (used for packaging of cement), weighing almost five kgs, carrying sharp-tipped stones and brick nuggets.

Background:

August 1997: Biul is born to Sakeena.

December 2001: Biul moves to Batamaloo from the bank of Zero Bridge, Raj Bagh with his mother and sister.

March 2002: Biul is admitted to the Government High School, Batamaloo.

July 2008: Biul went to school one morning and remained mysteriously absconding and missing for 17 days.

But now, when Biul sat watching the news about Obama on TV, there was a knock on the door. Biul's heart pounded.

They have come to take me, he thought. He stood in a corner of the room and put the TV on mute. When Sakeena went to answer the door, he strained his ears. The voice confirmed that it was the milkman. Biul sighed. Sakeena returned and marked the calendar, indicating that the milk had been delivered for the day. When she disappeared into the kitchen, Biul ran upstairs to the attic to scan the settlement, ensuring that everything seemed normal, that nobody else was coming to get him.

In autumn people loved basking outside their homes, soaking the last bit of sun to the point of boredom. The neighbourhood was a congestion of small, pillbox-like houses—the area divided by crisscrossing narrow dirt roads, the gables covered with corrugated tin, torn translucent polythene sheets or lines running across with clipped clothes drying on them, shutting off the view. The house facades were stuccoed or plastered or unplastered, the small lawns patterned in ways suggesting raw construction planning. The house that Biul and his family occupied was the succour provided by Dr. Imtiyaz after the government had failed to give Sakeena the promised rehabilitation in the Boatmen Colony, Bemina. Sakeena was still pursuing the case with the authorities.

It was a little colder in the attic. A lozenge of sunlight coming in through a hole in the tin roof warmed a spot on the back of Biul's hand. As he peered over the neighbourhood, he moved his hand and tried to give its other spots the opportunity to receive the warmth of the sun, as if washing his hand under a running tap.

Everything, as such, looked normal outside. Ghulam Muhammad Matta, the closest neighbour opposite Biul's house was roughly five metres away and yet quite close in the field of Biul's vision. He was as usual scaling the junk in his small compound packed with enormous piles of yellowed and mildewed newspapers and discarded plastic, his half-smoked cigarette tucked into the corner of his pursed lips, the smoke making him narrow his eyes and making him look more serious than he actually was. Past Ghulam Muhammad Matta's, another neighbour Nasreen was typically hunched over in the small blue window of her kitchen, peeking out at each passerby, spying on the ones she knew. Nobody had ever seen her anywhere else except in the frame of that window. Biul always wondered at this mystery.

Then there was Kousar Aunty, sitting behind her snot-nosed daughter in the gateway of their house, keenly searching through her greasy, dishevelled hair for lice. At the locality's end, close to the main road, a group of boys was playing carom. Occasionally, they shrieked with laughter, clapping their hands.

When Biul panned back to Ghulam Muhammad Matta, he noticed something more. There, beside Matta, was an open spreadsheet that showed a life-size image of a smiling black man who Biul recognized instantly. It is Obama, he said to himself. He swiftly descended the stairs, skipping alternate steps. In a matter of seconds, he was in Matta's small lawn, looking fixedly at the paper. It certainly was the president of the USA, the man he had been chasing on TV for the last few days. The superimposed text at the bottom of the image said:

Hon'ble US President Mr. Barack Obama, Welcome to World's Largest Democracy
Courtesy: Reliance India

'Can I have it?' Biul asked, gawking at the picture.

Ghulam Muhammad Matta stared at him in disbelief. It was the first time Biul had come into his lawn and talked to him. He wondered how Biul had come to know about the paper, and why on earth he wanted it. He kept his queries to himself and proffered the spreadsheet. 'Take it,' Matta said.

Back in the room, Biul sat cross-legged, staring at the picture. On TV, people with sickles in their hands were climbing coconut trees around the Gandhi Museum in Mumbai, one of the tourist venues Obama was going to visit. The men were going to harvest all the coconuts to prevent any accident. 'Authorities don't want to take a chance, since hundreds of people in India are injured or even killed by falling coconuts every year,' reported BBC.

Once more there was a knock on the door, a light pat, and Biul froze. This time it was Sakeena's mother. The moment he saw her, his palpitation subsided. Sakeena noticed the newspaper in front of Biul and wanted to ask him about it, but felt awkward to do so in front of her mother.

Biul slipped out of the house, quickly changing into a

pair of oversized flip-flops, half stumbling on the narrow cement path that ran around the house towards the backyard with the tin storeroom. He rummaged through barrels full of coal, pushing his hand behind a rusted tin trunk for a large flattened cardboard box. He pulled it out. His thumb scraped against the sharp corner of the trunk, but he ignored it, waiting for the gash to bleed. When it did, he sucked on it and plugged it with his forefinger, the blood sticky at first then quickly drying between his fingers.

He brought the cardboard to the front verandah and laid it flat on the ground. Then he cut the page featuring Obama out of the newspaper and glued it to the cardboard. He let it dry in the sun. Once dried, he found Sakeena's large scissors under her sewing machine and moved them along the outline of Obama's figure, cutting off the courtesy text. Here is the one—the most powerful, smiling, first black president of the USA—who will bring a ray of hope to Kashmir, thought Biul.

He swaddled the cut-out in the remaining newspaper and sneaked out of the gate, skittering towards Raja Photo Studio, excited and shivering with paranoia. This was the hour when Mohsin could usually be found alone at the photo studio.

When Biul was just metres away from Raja Photo Studio, he stopped and blinked in surprise. The display showcase seemed entirely changed, filled with photos of different models. The tin board overhead now read 'Mohsin Photo Studio'.

Mohsin was alone and seemingly free, seated at the large, glass-topped wooden counter where his uncle usually sat. He greeted Biul warmly and pulled a stool up for him.

'Is your uncle around?' Biul asked.

'No, he is no longer here.'

'Why? What happened?'

'This shop was actually my mother's legal share of the property. My uncle had taken it over after her death. Earlier, I was too young to know anything. A few months ago, my grandfather passed away, but not before legally securing the shop in my name. He called my uncle and extracted a written undertaking from him to leave the shop to me. It's going to be mine from next year, once I am eighteen. My uncle has pulled out in advance.'

'Good. But where do you live now?

'I live with one of my aunts.'

'Could you take a picture of me, please?' Biul asked.

'Sure. It'll be a pleasure to do it for free. What size do you want?'

'Normal size. But I need to pose with someone.'

They went into the studio. Biul unwrapped Obama. Mohsin was puzzled to see the cut-out.

'So it's him! The one everyone these days is talking about! Are you a fan?' Mohsin asked.

'A bit,' Biul said.

'Well, as you wish. But he won't appear as clear as you will in the picture.'

Biul dropped his arm over Obama's shoulder and posed.

'You both look good together,' Mohsin commented, holding the camera against his eyeline, adjusting the lens to focus well.

There were several clicks and flashes.

'Let Obama stay here for a few days, maybe more fans will turn up,' Mohsin told Biul.

'Please keep it,' Biul said.

'Thank you! I can give you the print of the photo now.'

The printer warmed and coughed up a sheet of glazy paper, issuing a wisp of pungent, powdery steam with identical photographs of Biul posing with Obama.

'Here you are,' said Mohsin, tucking the photographs into an envelope. 'Keep them all or keep the best one, your choice. All are yours.'

※

Biul strutted home, clasping the envelope. Worried, Sakeena had come out of the house to look for him. She saw him at a distance and her relief quickly changed to anger.

'What is this?' she asked, 'I thought they had come and taken you!'

He didn't respond, just fell into pace beside her.

She noticed the envelope in his hand but didn't question him about it, though she sorely wished to.

'I was just gone for a bit,' Biul said softly.

'It has been an hour or more,' she nagged. 'Tathi is worried. She has been waiting. I know you don't care.'

He hung his head in guilt.

In the evening, he showed the photographs to the big boys who huddled in groups in the playground. One of them teased Biul for being 'hypersensitive about the first black American president'. 'You are hyper. Don't worship the man; you never know … Don't die like this …' a boy said. The word 'hyper' disappointed Biul, but he was steadfast in his faith in Obama.

Days passed and finally Obama arrived in India. Biul clung to the TV, flipping from one channel to another, waiting for the breaking news. He followed each comment, speech, venture and visit of Obama and his wife, the First Lady Michelle, the couple's dance with a horde of poor schoolchildren in the premises of a rundown school building, waiting for the President to mention Kashmir. He sat up on those nights, gazing into the blue glow of the TV, the volume lowered to an indistinct mumble.

Biul spent some time pampering the glistening green necks of his pigeons in the lawn, stroking their rumps, throwing them into the air, their wings flapping before gaining height. They flew over the neighbourhood and came back, one by one, obeying his call, the coded whistles and calculated clapping. After shutting them in their coop, he made himself some kahwa and took the cup to the TV room.

It was the last day of Obama's tour in India. All the channels showed him live, making a speech in the Indian parliament. The president of the United States mentioned everything in his brief speech, praising Indian leadership, the country's economic might, heritage, civilization, the contribution of Zero, Gandhi and hospitality—'Indians unlocked the intricacies of the human body and the vastness of our universe'. It was all India, India and India. Kashmir wasn't mentioned at all.

Biul was supremely disappointed. Again, clear flashes of the policeman's dark hairy groin, clanking of the dangling, glinting steel buckle of his police belt, with a raised steel police logo on it, crossed his mind.

In the afternoon, Biul unplugged the TV and sat down to assist Sakeena in her tailoring, as he sometimes would. He sat calmly beside her, taking up a ladies' shirt. He stitched hooks onto its neck.

Later in the evening, he set off to Mohsin Photo Studio, his hands inside his pheran, sauntering, tearing the photographs he had taken with the cut-out of Obama into pieces and chucking them into the twilight like confetti. He dashed straight into the shop. Mohsin was busy with some customers at the counter outside, but he cut short his dealings to follow Biul, noting how upset he seemed.

Inside the studio, Biul stared at the cut-out of Obama. Then, deliberately, he slid it off its wooden holder. Mohsin stood in the doorway of the studio, watching him do it.

Biul replaced the cut-out with one of Salman Khan's that had been lying there for sometime.

Oil and Roses

To dwell is to garden.

—Martin Heidegger

The earth has to be at its softest to accept the seed well, thinks Gul Baaghwaan. He is planning to plant the hybrid seeds for the nth time. He has secretly thought of a name for the flower and plans to disclose it as soon as there is some sign of sprouting. He is confident that the flower will resemble a species which went extinct around sixty years ago in Kashmir.

Each spring the saplings tear through the earth, making Gul impatient and expectant. For years he has experimented only with the native nurseries. What he really wants, however, is to see riots of red poppies blooming everywhere against the green grass or the mustard crops of spring.

Gul is the head gardener at one of the terraced Mughal gardens in the Zabarwan hills in Srinagar. The hills and the gardens overlook the weedy Dal lake. Ever since he lost his only foster son to a stray bullet, Gul has grown serious, pernickety and reticent. When no one is looking, he talks to plants, trees, flowers and birds. And on their behalf, he responds to his own utterances.

Every morning, he whizzes down the shop-lined road from Braine to the garden on his new, shiny LML Vespa at full throttle. The scooter is a month old purchase, bought at the insistence of his wife. 'Now it suits your seniority in the garden,' she had said. Earlier, he had travelled up and down on his Atlas bicycle that now lies disused and idles in a shadowy tin shed at his house, its tyres deflated.

At home, Gul watches news on his colour TV set, pedastalled on a tin trunk near the hearth in the kitchen. His wife sits opposite the hearth on a *chowki* and cooks his piquant, tantalising favourite *gaada-tamaatar*. On the tiled wall of the chimney overhead is a picture of their dead son, Wahid. Other features in the kitchen include a disused hookah and a defunct Panasonic tape-recorder.

While sitting side by side with his wife in the evenings, Gul's wide and curious eyes are glued to the TV screen, fraught with grainy images of a furious crowd milling around Tahrir Square in Egypt. It is a visual from the Arab Spring.

Together, Gul and his wife struggle against their loneliness. Small tasks keep them busy. Either they garden in the ornamental patch of land in front of their house, or cultivate the small kitchen garden beside the house. Gul has a great variety of plants in his small garden: Sweet Williams, Fox Gloves, Yellow Poppies, red, yellow, white and pink rosebushes. Four equidistant bougainvillea-wound larches dot the four corners of the garden. A high wall of evergreens, cut into alternating troughs and crests, separate the ornamental garden from the kitchen garden, but a patch of rough grass seems to blend the two together. Gul himself is fond of a balance between the rough and fair. He doesn't approve of absolute trimmings or clear distinctions.

The kitchen garden is an irregular stretch of land, checkered with rectangular beds of collard greens, green chillies, knol khols and shallots. There is endlessly spreading mint, taking root beyond the edges of the land. Also, in a corner of the vegetation, near the compost dump, is a scaffolding made of rough wooden posts and crooked dry branches for bottle-gourds, bitter-gourds and cucumbers.

On Sundays and alternate evenings, Gul works part-time in the private gardens of the posh colonies of Ishbar and Nishat. Most of the palatial houses he goes to are uninhabited. In each one, he is guided by a watchman or a lone old man, and directed to tend this bed or that or prune this bush or that. He wonders about these vast houses. The emptiness and silence is broken only by the secretly darting birds who start warbling sweet music in the boughs of peach and pear and apple trees as soon as he begins to turn the earth inside out with his hoe or begins to hose down the turf.

Gul takes the second halves of Fridays off. First, he

mends his gardening tools, sharpens his shears and trowels and sorts through various species of seeds, wrapping them in pieces of the *Valley Times*. Then, after an early, light lunch, he takes his wife fifty kilometres away to a shrine at Chrar-e-Sharief, where, in the interstices of a wooden grille, he has tied a votive knot for his experimental flower to bloom. In the first decade of their childless marriage, Gul and his wife visited this shrine with great wishes, but in vain. Of late, she has now accepted her infertility and her foster son's tragic death, but her gardener husband has not given up hope.

*

On working days, when the sun begins to glare at the Mughal garden, Gul parks his Vespa inside the parking lot. In one of the shady corners of the garden, there is a shanty. Gul enters it and from a flaking Rexine kit he retrieves his old set of tools: a narrow trowel, a small garden hoe and a pair of long shears. He notes the time on his heirloom chain watch, slips it back into his waist-coat's pocket, takes the coat off, dusts its dandruff-covered shoulders and suspends it on a rusty nail, half dug into the wooden wall of the shanty. Then, as usual, he folds the sleeves of his Khansuit shirt and sets off towards the garden.

Out of habit, he takes a look at the *Valley Times*, delivered to the garden for the gardeners. He scans the headlines and then goes around, inspecting the work of his subordinates.

He never joins the superficial analysis of politics his colleagues indulge in during lunchtime, and always thinks of it as vague and petty, below his notice. Late in the morning, when springtime tourists start thronging the garden, Gul deliberately busies himself with tilling, trimming, pruning, shaping, sowing, watering, weeding and surveying the canopies of interspersing branches of chinars, observing the spaces between their dense, lush green foliage, filled with sunshine and shade. But he hardly smiles at blossoming flowers or happy tourists. He regards it all as his duty and never marvels at the fruits of his own labour. When alone and deep in the shrubbery, he begins talking to plants.

At the sight of tourists, he turns to the parched stream that used to flow down the centre of the garden in summer, dividing it into two equal parts. And strangely, he derives pleasure from its dryness. He becomes indifferent to the wind-fallen chinars, the long row of waterless fountains and the interiors of the medieval Mughal domes, littered with anonymous charcoal sketches of arrows-shot-through-hearts or knife-carved initials of lovers' names. But the discovery of discarded translucent bottles and empty chips packets irritates him. Even the photographers in the garden—those who woo the tourists with *cultural* fake silver jewellery, fake red velvet pherans and wicker trugs—irritate him. He hates the trespassers who ignore the fenced partitions in the garden to pluck flowers, despite the bright blue tin signages that scream: CUT A FLOWER AND YOU CUT A SMILE.

When the Army captains ferry jeeps full of their visiting families to the garden, he nearly curses them under his breath: *Aay'i yim haher!* And then he realizes the importance of acting like a family; the importance of a father's being a father to several tarrying children, a husband to a lovely and demanding wife, a son to his fragile old parents.

The wrath in Gul fizzles out, but the conviction remains.

After all his failed attempts to reproduce, Gul had adopted his nephew Showkat and raised him with all the love he would have lavished on his own child. Showkat had been the seventh son of Gul's elder sister who lived in a village seventy kilometres away and was a mother to eleven children: seven sons and four daughters. His sister had well understood Gul's desire for a child and so dedicated her last pregnancy to her childless brother.

Gul's wife had been a good mother to Showkat, but Gul himself had been an ideal father. He nursed Showkat as he nursed his gardens. He looked more of a mother than a father while nursing, caring and loving. 'If Showkat were a tree,' Gul once told his wife, 'I wouldn't need him to bear fruits. The shade would be enough for me.'

Showkat grew into a responsible youth. Shortly after earning his bachelor's in commerce, he got a clerk's job in a government department. For him and his parents, it was one of the greatest social and personal achievements in Kashmir. One day, on his way home from work, he passed an Army bunker at Batamaloo. At that very moment, a sudden tyre burst of a load-carrier truck occurred. The troops in the bunker instantly opened fire and shot indiscriminately at whoever was around. Showkat was one of those who died on the spot.

❧

Gul has had three decades to learn to tell one kind of tourist from another. He identifies them by the languages they speak. He can tell you about the Bengali winter tourists who visit the garden when there are still traces of snow and no flowers to see and smell, when the carpets of turf are still buff. He wonders why Bengali women protect their heads with thick bearskin caps, but wear nearly backless blouses under their sarees. He has watched these women steal mischievous glances at their family friends while their landscape-loving, scenery-smitten husbands take time capturing the sunset in their cybershot cameras. They wait the whole day to watch a lone shikara undulate on the glittering waves of the Dal lake at night.

Off and on, shy, newly married Indian couples turn up. There are frequent visitors—the Israeli groups, coming along with their heavy rucksacks, hiking up the precipitous Zabarwan terrains, mineral water bottles plunged into the elastic side-net-pockets of their bags. They come here looking for a shadowy place to fill their cigarettes with some mysterious powder.

Gul always feels tempted to warn the foreign tourists about the cheating guides, but ultimately he changes his

mind. He considers this his own form of revenge for
their arrival in his sacrosanct garden.

***

Back home, in the company of his wife, Gul remains
composed.

He watches the nightly news updates on TV, though
he prefers the lengthy BBC Urdu political analyses on
the radio.

Gul has witnessed every change in the valley of
Kashmir. Insurgency and counter-insurgency. And all
the *governance*.

Gul's wife offers him the walnut chutney she prepared
in the afternoon. He does not take it, his stomach is
upset.

After dinner, Gul and his wife continue to watch TV.
Tonight, the show is full of images of Gaddafi's severed
head.

***

The next day Gul is busy probing his experimental
hybrid saplings. Some spores have sprouted around their
tips. He observes the arrival of a large group of aged
spring tourists, men and women in orange caps, their
tops emblazoned with the words *Siddhi Vinayak* in red.
They do not seem interested in the garden but spending
more time staring at the local visitors.

Minutes later, while he examines a blunt lawnmower
and sniffs his palms for the smell of grass, he spots a

group of American tourists admiring a heart-shaped bed of roses near a sign that shouts AVOID TRESPASS. The group is accompanied by a local tour guide who interprets everything.

Gul recognizes the Americans from their accent. From the way they say 'goddamn' as 'gaaddamn'. *Haher!* comes first to his mind and even reaches the tip of his tongue. But he doesn't utter it.

After sometime he wipes his callused, soiled hands on his bum, clambers over a temporary fence constructed of green nylon-rope into the heart-shaped bed and shears off half a dozen dewed red and pink roses. He removes the thorns on the lower halves of the stalks and appears before the American group with a bunch of well-cut roses.

When he presents them, smiling for the first time at tourists, one of the Americans takes out his wallet from his back pocket and waves a hundred-rupee note in Gul's direction.

'No. Not money. All I wants a bit of attention, sir,' Gul says in broken English. 'We not have oil ... but we roses.'

The guide interprets and explains everything Gul says.

Gul opens the loosely furled fist of a blond American woman and carefully wraps her fingers around the bunched stalks. The woman and her companions look both pleased and baffled.

The day has grown bright. Gul has once again busied himself with the blunt mower, filing its twisted blades.

The number of tourists in the garden increases with each slow minute.

Gul is surprised by a pat on his back. He turns around, narrows his eyes to see the American lady he had presented the roses to. Gul drops the file and stands up reticently. 'Perhaps, there are more complicated things in this world than oil and roses. Aren't there?' the lady asks, smiling confidently. Gul nods. The lady strolls away.

Gul walks back to his hybrid saplings to properly observe the spores. Looking at them again might give him some idea of what they could bloom into, he thinks. Only time will tell.

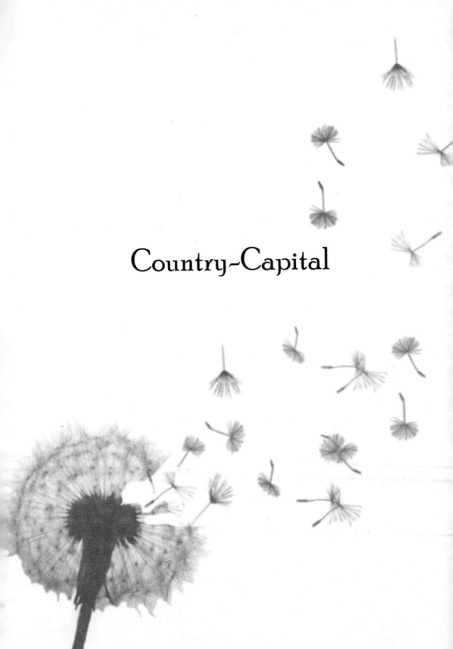

Country-Capital

Commitment is an act, not a word.
                              —Jean-Paul Sartre

It is a concrete building, the size of a normal village house. Built from sudden charity-like funds sanctioned under an educational scheme after a random visit from the zonal education officer, it stands on cattle-grazing land, disputed over by several local farmers: Muhammad Sultan Beigh, Ghulam Nabi Rather, Ghulam Hasan Dar and many others.

The classrooms are unplastered even on the inside and the upper-primary and middle divisions are still windowless. But the whole structure has a brand-new, shiny TATA-tinned roofing; so bright that it could lure a hovering aeroplane down from the heavens. The tin sheets run over a truss of fresh poplar rafters. The truss is naked on the inside and doesn't have a ceiling. It is due to the shade provided by the surrounding walnut trees that the tin doesn't become infernally hot during the summer.

Haji Nissar, the principal and an aspiring zonal education officer, a former core member of the local unit of Jama'at-e-Islami, has promised to return in the late afternoon, once he sorts out the trouble at his paddy field. Stray cattle are giving him a tough time, and then there is also this nuisance of sparrows that peck out the grains before they have taken any form on the crop. He wants two teachers to help him with the scarecrows and fencing. The teachers are supposed to stroll back to the school, their bitter willow *miswaaks* tucked deep into their cheeks, by late afternoon.

Mr. Manzoor Peer, the head master of the school, comes from Srinagar and has to burn litres and litres of expensive petrol in his 800 CC car (the students call it the 'matchbox'). This costs him half his monthly salary, and he seldom reaches on time. This doesn't even include the cost of maintenance for his car, especially for the torture the wheels undergo on the rutted, pitted road.

After he got the car washed at a workshop, someone cracked raw walnuts on its bumper while he was busy giving the principal and the village teachers lessons on how to run the school the city way.

In fact, Mr. Manzoor Peer has demanded a few days off—not any casual leave, though he has enough of them, unexhausted, in his account—and wants his attendance to be adjusted accordingly. Principal Nissar *understands* that Peer *needs* some time to get his newly built house tiled in Srinagar. Mr. Manzoor has recently broken off from his joint family. Haji Nissar has been pleased enough to grant the adjustment and has even offered to arrange for pure cedar wood, at a cheap rate, for the windows of Mr. Peer's new house.

So the command of the noisy class eight students passes to the self-designated head boy of the school. The head boy's face is scarred, suggesting how often he has fallen from walnut trees, and the stubborn brown dye of raw walnuts is yet to fade from his palms.

'Capital of Pakistan is?' he shouts at the confused class.

'India,' the voices respond in chorus, boys looking at each other for assurance of the correctness of their answer.

'Right! And Iran?'

'Am-rica,' the chorus roars.

It goes on like that till Captain Manohar Sumer of 122 Battalion Sadbhavna Rifles arrives, as usual, and overhears the class outside the shut door. And because he has arrived with a platoon of his AK-47-weilding men, the news of his arrival spreads through the village. The sarpanch—who doubles as a senior working member of the ruling party in the state—walks meekly into the vast compound of the school. He has a humped back. His hands are locked over his loins.

Captain, putting the flat palms of his hands together in respect, half rises at the sight of Sarpanch.

'I am so grateful for the rope-bridge,' Sarpanch says, still walking towards Sumer. 'The panch of the village across this dangerous stream is also very happy with it. He wanted me to convey his thanks to you.'

'Pleasure,' says Sumer, 'all my pleasure.'

'And, of course, the free eye camp was also very impressive. Jaana can see now. It's like Taaja's cataract didn't exist at all. And we have just begun praying in the new mosque.'

'Thank you,' Sumer feels overwhelmed.

'Yes, yes, and the radio sets are too good. Right from my childhood, I have been told that Philips is a quality brand. I say that any damn thing from the Army canteen supply is bloody good. Bloody original. Everything.'

'You are always welcome,' Sumer says.

The country-capital exercise chorus of class eight finally reaches their ears.

'They seem to believe every country's capital is either India or Am-rica. Bloody morons. They have to learn,' Sarpanch, embarrassed by the students, tries to please Sumer when he looks in the direction the voices are coming from.

When the two-kilo iron hammer pounds on the thick round plate of iron, and the principal and teachers have returned to join Sarpanch and Captain Sumer, an uncontrollable flood of young boys comes spilling out of different holes. They wear rubber flip-flops or black plastic winter shoes or torn canvas shoes or unpolished black leather school shoes, and are uniformed in cobalt blue pants and sky blue shirts.

'Basically, I have come with a new proposal,' says Sumer, after all the boys have rushed past. 'We want the sixth and seventh grades spared for Bharat Darshan, All India tour.'

'Nothing like that, Sir. Whenever,' responds Sarpanch.

'*Bilkul bilkul!*' the submissive voices of the principal

and other two teachers follow even before Sarpanch has finished expressing his consent.

꙳

'Put all the cedar into the Volvo, the same one we're using to take the kids,' Sumer instructs his men. 'Its belly is big enough to carry more than a hundred pieces. And put the kids' luggage and other things over them.'

The long aerials of the jammer on the vehicle wag in the air as the Rakshak tries to whiz away on the rutted track. A doll-like pink Sai Baba sits in the middle of the dashboard with his tiny hand raised, blessing all.

'And if these adamant Bakarwaals raise queries or try to arm-twist us about the stumps in the forest, blame this on the bastard detained in the south camp barrack. Say that besides others things, he was a smuggler too. And, in addition, ask if these are the ethics behind the so-called "movement",' the captain continues and laughs.

꙳

Sarpanch wears a new white Khansuit and his farmer's cap looks washed clean, except for an odd grease stain. He has been given a green flag to wave at the Volvo full of shrieking excited boys who have hardly ever been to Srinagar, let alone on a Bharat Darshan.

Sarpanch waves the flag and a loud clap follows as the Volvo begins to chug.

꙳

Mr. Manzoor Peer surfs channels on his colour TV until he reaches the government news channel.

He glares at the close-up of a boy in a navy blue tracksuit and a matching cap that says:

Sadbhavna Force
122 Bn

In the background, there is a big cherry-red plush bus whose flat-faced bonnet is covered in a banner that boasts:

Watan Ki Sair
Aman Ki Yatra
(A journey around the nation
A journey of peace)

'... Ummm ... we were very happy ... are happy ... We are very happy indeed to ... ummm ... thankful to Army's 122 battalion ... that ... ummm ... that has provided us with this opportunity to see our country ...' says a student in a sound bite.

'*Haraamzaada!* Shabeer Najaar of sixth grade. Beggars for crumbs,' Mr. Manzoor Peer cusses under his breath.

'We had never seen Taj Mahal, Qutab Minar and Red Fort ... We are very thankful to Captain Sahab who brought us here to see these beautiful things ...' continues Shabeer Najaar, narrating it all in the same way he narrates mugged-up lessons at school.

'Captain Manohar Sumer. Say the full name, *saalay*!' yells Sumer, lying sozzled in his bed, swilling the last pint as he watches it all on his wall-mounted LCD in the Army camp.

'We also saw the Parliament. We had earlier seen it only on the fifty-rupee notes our fathers used to pay the seed sellers in the village. We took a ride on the metro. There are long green buses everywhere and plain wide roads. Something we don't have in the village ...'

'*Waah!* Sarpanch's class seventh grandson too. *Haraamzaada* once broke the side mirror ... Enough is enough! I cannot work in this school of collaborators and traitors!' Mr. Manzoor Peer thinks, chewing on an expletive.

Mr. Manzoor Peer's family surrounds him in the room. His wife sits cross-legged in a corner, doing strawberry pink embroidery along the border of a white shawl, her biannual devotional present to Mirwaiz Molvi Umar, a separatist leader. Her golden-rimmed glasses are slipping down to the tip of her nose. She curses the Social Welfare Department for withholding her salary for the last three months. She moves her lips as if muttering holy words.

Peer's children, a boy and a girl who study in the local missionary school, write chits to each other about something while pretending to do their homework. A large part of the floor is littered with their textbooks, notebooks, schoolbags, chewed rubber-topped pencils and items from their geometry boxes. The boy stealthily pricks his sister with the compass over a silent joke and sets her screaming. Disturbed and disgusted, Mr. Manzoor Peer glares at them.

When the boys return from Bharat Darshan, the school is already open.

The boys have an air about them now. They find it hard to relate to their village and its people.

The sarpanch and the principal have stationed some boys with garlands in the school compound for the reception of the returning students. There is a special garland for the captain too.

'Welcome! Welcome! Welcome!' says the sarpanch, approaching the captain with a wide smile.

The pleasantries and greetings are exchanged. Parents hug their sons as if they have returned from Haj.

'Welcome! Now, one more thing ...' Sarpanch says, smiling widely, putting the garland around Sumer's thick, dusky, oily military neck. 'Please keep in mind the coming panchayat elections.'

'Of course! Of course!'

The principal has returned to his office, but Sumer and Sarpanch are still deep in conversation out in the compound. Meanwhile the class eight students' chorus has begun reiterating the country-capital exercise.

'Capital of Jammu and Kashmir?' screams the head boy.

'India!' the chorus confidently responds.

Shabaan Kaak's Death

Morning or night, Friday or Sunday, made no difference, everything was the same ... What did days, weeks or hours matter?
        —Leo Tolstoy, *The Death of Ivan Illych*

We say that the hour of death cannot be forecast, but when we say this, we imagine that hour as placed in an obscure and distant future. It never occurs to us that it has any connection with the day already begun or that death could arrive this same afternoon, this afternoon which is so certain and which has every hour filled in advance.
        —Marcel Proust, *In Search of Lost Time*

He wasn't easily convinced of the size and space of his grave. For some days now, he had been doodling on a stray piece of paper, holding—in his trembling, speckled, bony hand—one of his great-grandson's eraser-topped stub of a pencil, drawing a grave.

Shabaan Kaak was the oldest person in Hawal, and widely revered in the heart of Srinagar's downtown. He had three sons, six daughters, twenty-three grandchildren and three great-grandchildren. His wife had been thirteen years younger than him and had died years ago from

tuberculosis. His eldest son was a retired overseer and
the youngest a Class-A contractor of construction. The
middle one, Dr. Imtiyaz Ahmad, was a psychiatrist who
lived at Raj Bagh, some eight kilometres from Hawal, in
a separate house, with his small family. Shabaan Kaak
had seen a lot in life, which was fraught with both sense
and nonsense, and lived through the strangest of times.
In his last few days, he was very nearly content.

Along with a property will, Shabaan Kaak handed the
map of his ancestral graveyard to his eldest son. With
neatly pencilled arrow marks, the map indicated exactly
where Kaak's grave ought to be dug. Also, the map
showed the geometric dimensions of the trench and the
lahad, the vault, of the grave.

Aged a hundred and two, Shabaan Kaak would often
say: *Hati heor gasi insaan pan'ni marzi marun* (above
hundred one must die at one's will). One morning,
when one of his grandsons told him about the death of
a teenager hit by an expired teargas shell on the Hawal
crossway, Kaak blurted: *Baasaan chhu Khuada saebas
chhus ba mashith goumut* (looks like God has forgotten
only me). But most often he would wish and pray: may I
die on a sunny Friday.

He also believed: All Kashmiris know me, know how
old I am, and that there couldn't be less than, at least, ten
thousand men at my funeral prayers.

He had witnessed all the major political and social

events, changes and upheavals in Kashmir. The rise and fall of cruel monarchs and charismatic political leaders, each India-Pakistan tussle over Kashmir. He had seen famous legends, borne witness to historic treaties and understood the fickle temperaments of several public figures and politicians. He had seen how some revolutionary events had become cyclic, how true legends and old sacrifices would come back time and again. He had observed that it was the common man and the good leader who truly mattered in the circus of power, that it was their own deeds that shone on in public memory. And finally, he had come to the conclusion that nothing was more important than a return to God. He was more faithful to God than religion could have made him.

All his great-grandchildren spoke in Urdu, so Shabaan Kaak had to struggle with his broken Urdu, always funnily mixed with Kashmiri words: *Asal kami karni aastaa hai! Ikhlaaq saan jado-jehat karin aasta hai aur Khuadayas zaarpaar karun aastaa hai! Bas mein aur kuch nahin dapta hui!* (Good deeds, struggle-with-ethics and God is what I preach; rest is all farce!), he would say at least one hundred times a day. The children giggled at his sayings, but he ignored that and maintained the same formula until his death. In his old heart, he had forgiven almost everyone who had caused him harm in his long life.

Shabaan Kaak had also always prayed for an 'easy death', but more than that he was conscious about dying on a sunny Friday and having a minimum of ten thousand men at his funeral. He fell slightly ill for a few days before he passed away. Just slightly.

✺

Kaak died at the start of a strict curfew imposed in the city following the killing of a schoolchild hit on the head by a teargas shell. The curfew would last a week.

It was ten-thirty in the morning of a long Thursday in July. The silent lamentation took place in the grand old house. Prevented by the severe curfew, his middle son Dr. Imtiyaz could only call his brothers over the phone and enquire about the progress of the funeral. The cellphones in the old house would ring time and again and sometimes nobody would pick up the call. Then Kaak's middle son would call his nephews to ask about the funeral. 'Hello! Hellooooo! When are you giving him the final bath? … Okay … Has the shroud come? … Okay … Will the Army and police allow you to take him to the graveyard? … Okay,' he asked all these questions.

Shabaan Kaak was old enough to be noisily mourned. Given the curfew, his sons could barely arrange for a tailor to stitch their father a proper shroud. There was nowhere to find the particular white cloth he deserved. Nowhere to find myrrh to scent the bathwater for Kaak's *gosul*, the final bath. In desperation, his daughters-in-law disarranged all the hung, folded and well-ironed clothes in the wardrobes and old tin trunks, searched through every bureau or drawer or hanging wicker basket in the house, looking for a ball of camphor in vain. Ultimately, it was borrowed from a neighbour. Fortunately the local mosque was only a few metres away, so Shabaan Kaak's grandsons brought the *taabood*, the bier, home.

When the body was ready for burial, Kaak's sons sobbed and wailed, not particularly for the loss of their father's soul, but out of worry for what would happen if they were not allowed to take the body to the graveyard for burial.

The vantage points of the main road were littered with large stones, spiky barricades or coils of razorwire; bevies of policemen and Army soldiers patrolled in riot gear, holding transparent shields and swinging transparent canes, as if dressed to play some odd game, something between cricket and rugby.

Gradually, and with the help of some neighbours, Kaak's sons somehow managed to talk about the matter to a police officer stationed outside the colony. After an hour of pleading with him, Kaak's sons were allowed a maximum of ten men to accompany the body to the graveyard.

Shabaan Kaak's funeral prayer was offered in a narrow lane outside the old house. The lane couldn't accommodate more than two short rows of men. So only twenty-two men offered the *janaaza*. The Molvi sahab of the local mosque was on leave, so a neighbour had to lead the prayer. Later, the same neighbour would offer the *fateha* at the grave, full of mistakes in the recitation, and it would become evident that the funeral prayer too had not gone well.

Finally, two of Kaak's sons, five grandsons and three neighbours carried the bier, covered in a green velvet pall, to the ancestral graveyard. The weight of the bier was much greater than that of the body. Sometimes, while carrying it to the graveyard, his sons even doubted their father's presence inside the box. They wondered if they were bearing an empty *taabood* on their shoulders.

The sunless sky and the swelter of midsummer were making the late afternoon stuffy. The two most prominent sounds in the breathless air were either the sirens of police vehicles or the concert of diverse birdsong, something normally drowned out by the daily din of traffic and anxious human hubbub. Since Ghulam Rasool, the gravedigger, belonged to the other side of Hawal and couldn't be reached, Kaak's sons and grandsons had to dig the grave themselves, something they had never imagined having to do. The first rectangular pit they dug was shallow and the vault couldn't even bear the weight of one human being over it. It crumbled. Then they moved to another side of the graveyard, where, if he were alive, Shabaan Kaak would never have wanted to be buried: under the shade of an acacia tree. The level of the earth here was lower than that of the first spot. This pit began to fill with water as soon as it had been dug.

They threw the mud back into the pit and moved to another side of the graveyard where there was a sprawling bank of irises. At once they again began to turn the earth inside out. Being inexperienced at digging, Shabaan Kaak's sons and grandsons sweated, panted and cried.

Again, it was not because they had just lost their father. Instead, they were worried about whether this pit too would fill with water and prove useless.

At last Shabaan Kaak was irrevocably buried.

Late in the night it drizzled. The next day being Friday, the order for a stricter curfew had been bellowed across the city.

The House

*It may be that the satisfaction I need depends on
my going away, so that when I've gone and come
back, I'll find it at home.*

—Rumi

*so I wait for you like a lonely house
till you will see me again and live in me.
Till then my windows ache.*

—Pablo Neruda

*Some lesser husbands built a latrine on the
hillside.*

—V S Naipaul, *A House for Mr. Biswas*

Mir Manzil is in disorder but lively.

The maidservant Taja's daughter's family lives in two rooms on the ground floor. One room has been given to Gulzar Ahmad, the neighbourhood poultry-seller. Sacks full of chicken feed and new lots of broilers are neatly stocked in the room with two large, netted windows for good ventilation. The bare cement floor is covered with droppings all over.

Another room on the same floor is used for weekly social gatherings.

A corridor divides the second floor into half. One half belongs to Ghulam Nabi Mir and the other to two students, Zubair and Ishfaq. Ghulam Nabi shifted to Mir Manzil in 1995. The two students moved in right after him.

No one is a tenant in the house.

Farooq Ahmad Mir, the owner of the house, himself lives on the second floor. There are six rooms on his floor. His second paternal-cousin Ghulam Nabi Mir has stowed half of his household paraphernalia in two of the six rooms, even though he lives in an old house in Nawa Kadal with his family. His own house dates back to the period of Dogra rule in Kashmir. Time has made it creaky and rickety. He needed a small but new house and had initiated construction of one in Bemina, but after marrying his two daughters off, he has found himself heavily in debt. He couldn't finish building the new house and so, he transported half of his household stuff to Mir Manzil.

Three rooms on the second floor of Mir Manzil belong to Farooq's three children—two sons and a daughter—who live abroad. They visit home occasionally, each one at a different time, so the siblings don't see each other much. The elder son Aabid is studying management in Sydney. He visits home in midsummer. The middle child, Aasiya, was sent to Bangalore to study medicine, but was discovered living in Dubai without any degree in medicine. Farooq has never properly understood how, why and when she landed in Dubai, or what exactly she is doing there. She has not explained either. He refrains from digging too deep, afraid that she will get upset and refuse to visit him. She comes in January for a fortnight or so, spends very little time with her father and more time out of the house. She goes out on one or the other pretext, returns late at night, trying not to *disturb* him. Then she goes to her room and plays Taylor Swift at a high volume.

Farooq's youngest son, Aarif, comes once every three or four years. He was sent to Moscow for a degree in medicine like his sister, but he fell in love with a Russian salesgirl and left the course midway to marry her. He is always accompanied by his wife and two blonde children. On each visit, he becomes a translator-cum-interpreter between his father and his family, translating and interpreting Kashmiri concerns and affections into Russian and endless Russian queries and appreciations into Kashmiri.

Since his wife Zareena's death, Farooq has never been to the attic on the third floor. Only Taja takes care of the mice-bitten, dusty stacks of mattresses and quilts and blankets and stockpiles of copper utensils, stored in large tin trunks, and all the other odds and ends in the attic.

The two twin bathrooms outside the house are for the use of strangers. The vast compound in front of the house is almost always busy, hosting either a wedding banquet under a marquee or a condolence meeting. Except for a few withering larches and a single unattended weeping-willow, the garden in the compound is bare yet dotted everywhere with tarpaulin sheets smothered by slices of bottle gourds or tomatoes or brinjals—vegetables that the neighbours have scattered to dry in the sun and would store them for use in winter. A wide terracotta path separates the garden from the compound wall. The neighbours find space for their loaned cars on this path at Mir Manzil. The nearest neighbours take frequent liberties in drying their washed laundry on the compound walls. One of the neighbours has even broken the wall to the east of the house and made a shortcut into it to avail the utilities of Mir Manzil.

Unlike old times, the house is now always illuminated and full of noise, abuzz with laughter, bickering, screams, cheeping of Gulzar's chickens, occasional wails of Taylor Swift, cheer of weddings and humming condolences.

Mir Manzil was once known as the greatest wonder in all of Bulbul Bagh. Farooq Ahmad Mir was the first and the only gazetted government officer in the area. He was the only son of his parents and had inherited a great deal of land. His mother had passed away when he was sixteen. A year after he married Zareena, when he was twenty-five, his father passed away as well. Zareena proved to be a responsible and loving wife and some consolation for the loss of his parents. When Aarif was born, Farooq decided to build a new house in place of his ancestral one. The house he built was the highest, four-storey building in Bulbul Bagh. It was stuccoed on three sides and its façade stood distinct with its white rough-cast. All its large windows were arched on the top and painted in a dark shade of brown. A black plaque at the gate pompously boasted 'Mir Manzil'.

Farooq was the richest, most reputed, most influential, most arrogant, most stubborn, most envied and most hated person in the neighbourhood. His house looked like an extension of all that he was. People who passed by the grand house would marvel at it and wish that they could take a tour through it. Everyone had his or her own imagination of its interior: colours and shades of the walls, wardrobes, furniture, carpets, curtains, vases—everything.

Zareena had always been opposed to the ideas of grandeur and pomp. Contrary to Farooq's tastes, moods and beliefs, she was a warm soul, very social and benevolent. Though she came from a family which was a dozen times wealthier than her husband's, she was modest in all her tastes. Yet she and Farooq loved each other deeply.

People rarely had access to the house, and those who had been to its drawing room—where Farooq, dressed in a long embroidered tweed gown, would attest their papers or listen to their grievances and hardly ask them if they wanted a glass of water or a cup of tea—always wanted to see the rest of the place, stealing glances at whatever they beheld while entering and leaving. Those who had never been to the house would interrogate those who had and demand descriptions and would then fantasize about it. Many couldn't even dream of having a home as grand as Mir Manzil.

Zareena kept the house lively. Unlike Farooq, who wanted the house to be grand and yet inhospitable, Zareena would try to draw people in. Every Friday morning, she appeared at the gate with a platter full of *taher*, rice sautéed in turmeric, shallots and salt, and serve it to the passersby. She would stay there at the gate with Taja behind her, long after she would be done distributing the *taher*, and smile all the while. Every neighbour was as happy with Zareena as he or she was annoyed by Farooq.

Farooq's children grew up the way he determined them to. They would never interact or play with the neighbourhood kids. They inherited a superiority complex from their father, which made them feel different and more special than the other children. They played with each other indoors and would barely step out of the gate. Against Zareena's wishes, they followed in their father's footsteps.

❦

One fateful day in May 1991, two insurgents attacked an Army patrol outside Mir Manzil and escaped through the compound of the house. They ran across it, jumping over the wall at the other end, disappearing into the dense neighbourhood. After hearing the gunshots, Farooq and Zareena rushed out of the house to bolt the gate. Taja had been visiting her house in another neighbourhood and the three children were busy doing their homework. But before they could reach the gate, the Army was already inside the compound, furious and desperate. The troops fired indiscriminately and Zareena was hit.

The next morning, Farooq found himself lying on a bed in the Intensive Care Unit of the Bone & Joint Hospital, surrounded by his relatives, some friends, his eldest son, neighbours and a team of doctors. He had been hit by two bullets in his left arm.

Healing slowly from the bullet injuries, for a month he kept asking about his wife and every time he was told that his wife was alive and was being treated in another hospital. Slowly, as the days passed, he realized that people were lying to him and that his wife was dead.

Days, months and years passed. Farooq's wounds healed, the political and social situation in Kashmir changed drastically. Without Zareena, Farooq's family began to disintegrate and he grew more and more lonely, frustrated and deeply forlorn. He missed Zareena and would often stay indoors and cry secretly in her memory. By this time, several houses in the neighbourhood were rising as high as Mir Manzil. Soon, it was no longer the most opulent or tallest house in Bulbul Bagh.

Then came a time when Farooq saw off, one by one, all three of his children. He lavished huge sums of his savings on their education and living expenses.

In his aggravated loneliness and frustration, Farooq

Mir would pace from one room to another, without
purpose. He would aimlessly run up and down the stairs.
He lost interest in everything. He began to be irregular
at his work.

He would spend all evening watching TV in his room.
After the news, he would watch lawn-tennis matches,
and even the late night special news bulletins for the deaf
and dumb. Unable to sleep, he read outdated magazines
and newspapers, stroking his left arm the whole while.
Years after the bullet injuries had healed, the arm still
ached sometimes.

Gradually, Farooq began venturing out of the house,
surprising the neighbours. He began idling at Gulzar's
poultry shop. Once, in the course of a conversation,
Gulzar mentioned the smallness of his shop and moaned
that it had insufficient space for the chickens and their
feed. He said that he was looking for space nearby to
station new lots of chickens until he sold those in the
shop. Farooq offered one of the rooms on the ground
floor of Mir Manzil.

Taja had not been coming to the house for some time.
It worried Farooq. The day she returned, she cried all
the while, narrating how confused and indecisive she
had felt while resolving a problem at her own home. Her
daughter, her son-in-law and their three small children
had been thrown out of their house for some reason.
Taja's daughter and her family were homeless now
and Taja was already running out of space at her own
house. Her two sons and their large families were living

in a house of two rooms and sharing a single common kitchen. They were reluctant and unable to accommodate their sister and her family.

Farooq came up with a solution. He offered two rooms and a bathroom of Mir Manzil to Taja's daughter and her family.

Farooq started attending the local mosque. Insomniac that he was, he would even wake up for *tahjud*, the extra prayers offered in the middle of the night. He grew a long beard. With time, he began taking an interest in the Bulbul Bagh Mosque Management Committee's meetings and Bulbul Bagh's social matters. Soon he became an active member of the Mosque Management Committee. People started frequenting Mir Manzil to seek Farooq's advice on personal matters. Farooq dedicated a room on the ground floor to weekly social gatherings and the Committees's meetings. He presided over matters regarding marriage disputes, property issues and divorces.

He couldn't bear the destruction of his cousin Ghulam Nabi Mir's house in Nawa Kadal and immediately offered him a major part of the second storey in Mir Manzil. The other half was offered to the two students Zubair and Ishfaq, who, having come to the city for studies, once came to Mir Manzil, looking for a room to rent. Farooq not only offered them a room each, but, treating them as his own children, he told them that they could stay in his house for as long as they wished.

All those who had taken refuge in the house lived

there for free, much to the contentment of Farooq
Ahmad Mir. With all these people around, Farooq felt
secure and engaged. Now and again he would either visit
Taja's daughter on the ground floor and play with her
children or he would visit the students on the first floor,
asking them if they were comfortable, if they needed
anything from him and if the power and water supplies
were functioning smoothly.

It is a Sunday morning and dozens of neighbourhood
elders have gathered in the house to discuss a land dispute.
Ghulam Ahmad Parray and Wali Mohammad Bhat have
had a prolonged conflict over a piece of land in Bulbul
Bagh that actually belongs to another neighbour whose
claims have always been stifled. Everyone is curious to
know Farooq Ahmad Mir's opinion on the issue. But he
is eager to proceed for a resolution only after the ignored
neighbour is acknowledged.

Some Small Things I Couldn't Tell You

How do I know what I think until I see what I say?

—E.M. Forster

Dear son,
I am writing this in a hurry. I have tried to be as elaborate and sensible as possible in the time I have stolen from your mother to write this. Since she is off to get morphine for me and since we have sent you to your grandparents' home for sometime to keep you as much unaware of my health as possible, I am using this opportunity to write to you.

Dear son, I'll be gone when you read this. You will inherit all the books in my library—perhaps you will find this letter then.

There are a few things I have not told you, partly because you were too young to understand them. I will tell you those things now.

What's going to happen to me doesn't make any difference to me. I died the day when certainty dawned on me. When I wished I were illiterate ... I could read all my reports ... (most of the times ignorance is better than awareness, more than bliss; reminds me of Kant: 'whosoever increaseth knowledge increaseth pain').

In the beginning, after I came to know about the lump in the right lobe of my lungs, I wanted to beg desperately of everyone: save me! I didn't want to sound childish. Even when at the same time I knew I had become a child within myself. I can't swing between avoidance of people and a need for engagement, can't tell you how absurd now the television in my room appears to me, how abstract the programmes. At the time when one knows that one isn't going to see a certain thing again, one wants to hate looking at it, but at the same time you can't avert your eyes for the thing, the sight, a scene engages you—the reddish characters in the flawed soap operas. I swing between the avoidance and engagement. I want more and more people to come and meet me back to back, even if they talk nonsense. I'd now enjoy that too. Earlier it was hard for me to tolerate the irrational and superficial commentary of my ordinary neighbours and naïve colleagues over petty things. Now I want to be engaged all the time, by anyone, without a break; I want to be absorbed in talk and save myself from brooding on my death and its certainty. (These days I am frequently reminded of Jack Nicholson's dialogue from *The Bucket List*: 'Somewhere, some lucky guy is having a heart attack ...' What a precise calculation! Never watch the movie, please.)

The other day, after your mother learnt that the lump in me has begun to spread its agents to the other parts of my body and certain things have sprouted in my brain, she slapped her face and beat her chest. Then, wearing a fake smile, pretending otherwise—the rashes from the slapping still visible around her neck—she quickly came over to where I was lying and asked me if I'd like to have a cup of kahwa. I agreed and ignored her beating herself. I knew that ignoring her self-abuse was the wisest course for us, otherwise she might just do it in front of me and punish us both that way. But, vaguely, I still tumbled into morose utterances, told her that the little pillow she wanted to slip behind my head to keep my neck upright and relaxed and easy was of no use, as I had already begun heading to have a sunbaked brick as my pillow inside the dark vault of my grave.

My spasms are gradually subsiding under the morphine these days. I can't tell you how terrified I am of the night, of dreams and sleep.

My oncologist is scarier than my cancer. He shocks me more than any news of death. The way he shakes his head from side to side and sucks his lips when he looks at my reports—it kills me a thousand times. I want to tell him to counsel me even though I know how ineffective any counselling is for a patient like me. So I've told your mother that I no longer want to visit the oncologist. I want to die in peace.

Today, I went for the final dose of chemo. Your mother began discussing ifs with me, starting with *if* I hadn't smoked, I wouldn't have been going to the hospital like this. *If* I had accepted the financial help of her paternal cousin, I'd have been all right. (By the way, do you remember the toys Syed Hishaam-ud-Deen Naqshbandi, your mother's paternal cousin, the then Deputy Superintendent of Police of Srinagar, had brought for you? Toys that you found broken into pieces later?)

❧

I was born into a farming family. My mother was illiterate, my father semi-educated. But my younger sister (your aunt) and I received an adequate education. I couldn't thank God enough for the social background he had given me. It gave me perspective of the kind that someone born into a protective, elite family never receives. That kind of background allows you to be grounded in the realities of life, I feel.

I grew into an earthy boy, surrounded by the smells and scents of our family farm: of vegetables, grass, soil, well water and sweat. I have not learnt as much at school as I did at the baker's, the barber's and the butcher's shops. Those were the real sites of knowledge. I did enjoy my share of pampering. I was the first boy in the neighbourhood to have a red Hero Ranger, with side-mirrors on both sides of its straight steering, the spokes of its wheels embellished with multicoloured plastic beads—things envied in the entire locality. I was so lucky to not become like Aarif, our neighbour's only son, always locked up in his house, never allowed to play with the neighbourhood kids, never allowed to venture out. He eventually grew into a sissy, listless about the world, easily intimidated by gangs of rowdy kids on the street or even by the sight of a calm dog. Every kid's childhood at least includes catching butterflies, attempting to trap sunlight, splashing water, jumping off trees—and countless other nonsensical things. But I doubt Aarif had any such joy.

I had fun with my cousins, stealing fruit from the plum orchards. We relished the chase and abuse of the owners. Sometimes we would bunk school to go swim in the local stream, basking and gossiping on its sandy banks. Once we were startled by our parents wielding long sheaves of nettle, all set to punish us. We were taken naked to our homes, paraded through the neighbourhood. The shame it brought was worse than the lashes we received later. We tried to earn our own money by ploughing other people's land and making five rupees per bed; once I made forty rupees in a single day. We'd make paper bags from old newsprint and sell them to shopkeepers. We collected the remains of copper wire, burned off the insulation, wound the bits around pebbles into balls and traded them to Ghulam Muhammad Misgar, the neighbourhood coppersmith.

We'd even make kites, display them on the facades of our houses, attract the other neighbourhood kids and then sell them at an enviable profit.

I thank God for the gifts of curiosity and creativity that I inherited from my mother. I had a toolkit of my own: a small hammer, a saw, rusty fragments of an hacksaw-blade, an awl (which I'd use for binding books too), a hand drill, a multipurpose screwdriver, pliers, scissors, a pouch full of nails, screws, tacks, nuts, bolts, valves of different sizes. I'd go about our house, or sit in the attic, making and mending things. I'd make *chowkis*, wooden table lamps, writing desks, ironing boards, coops (for our chicks and ducklings) and guns too. I miss all that sorely, all those little wonders, those bruises, those blisters and gashes on my hands. There truly is nothing like childhood.

Enjoy yours as much as possible.

You've had a different upbringing from mine, a little more sophisticated than mine. Even though you don't wander into the same classrooms as I did—the baker's, the butcher's, the barber's—I hope you will walk barefoot when nobody is looking, feel the pebbles and the coarseness of earth prod your soles. This will relieve you of your worldly pains. Do it while you are still a child, before reality tries to push you into a new phase where weaknesses and handicaps are not forgiven. Where you have to sound more accountable than reasonable. The real love is less emotional, more mechanical and constant and sustainable enough. The second name of love is responsibility. It is above sacrifice. Rather, it's sacrifice itself.

I got married to your mother soon after I found a job with a good newspaper. Syed Hishaam-ud-Deen Naqshbandi, your uncle, didn't support our relationship (don't ask me to go into the details of how we came to know each other; confessions mostly ruin and rarely help anyone), but he couldn't do anything to stop it.

He could have made me 'disappear' in police custody or simply kill me, but my profession saved me. Once your mother and I were married, he changed his strategy and behaviour, and started to patronize us. Your mother wouldn't believe what I told her about him then, but now, like every second citizen of Srinagar, she does. That he is a killer, a mass murderer. There was a time when your mother wanted you to become a police officer like him when you grew up. But I'd say, let Afzal become anything, even push a cart in Lal Chowk, but don't ever wish for him to become anything like his uncle. Your uncle will *outlive* me, maybe he'll outlive all of us (we saw him on TV the other day, giving lectures on social morality, ethics and Islam; he still looks younger than me, doesn't he?), and he doesn't even smoke.

Your mother and I got along very well. She turned out to be a very loving, possessive and adamant wife. She sold all her jewellery to expand our one-storey house into a three-storey building. I insisted on not expanding the house, said that I didn't want it to become like a typical house in a posh colony, a house which looks like an extension of the inhabitant's mindset: opulent, extravagant, expansive, obscene. But she said that she was doing it out of love, lavishing all her savings on building a home for us.

In a second instance, she took up arms against the neighbours opposite ours over a stream that once ran between our compounds. It belonged to both of us and ought to be equally divided between the two families, but they had claimed the whole thing. It was now dry and we could no longer divide it. They had sown poplars along its length. I had never felt compelled to solve this dispute. Your mother, however, was not so easily deterred and she filed a case in court. But she also prevented me from tending to the ornamental garden I had set up on what should have been our side of the stream. She still doesn't allow me to work there, and wants me to wait for a legal decision on the property. But I am asking you now: please do tend the garden after I go, no matter how long it takes to settle the dispute. Just because one doesn't live to see settlements and solutions doesn't mean that you should quit striving for better things on your side.

Son, many of us are consumed by our egos. The day we conquer our ego is the day we win ourselves and that is when we win the world. But we should take care not to compromise on our sense of justice. Being humble doesn't mean you have to please *all*.

I think your mother is back, for I can hear her parking the car. If you're still wondering how those toys your uncle brought for you broke and became defunct, let me tell you ... No, it wasn't our loyal maid, though we blamed her every time. It was me who broke them. Yes, I broke those toys. It would have been difficult for you to understand why I destroyed them secretly; it would have struck as being odd to you. You might have despised me then. But now I hope you are mature enough to understand that I was trying to protect you from the shadows of evil love.

May God protect you! May you live long, spread justice and love! But however long you live, never lose yourself to the pleasures of life. Remember that one day we all have to die and justify our lives before Allah. *Innaa lillaah'i wa innaa ilai'hi raaji'uun.* To God we belong and to Him we shall return.

The Silent Bullet

The human mind cannot be absolutely destroyed with the body, but something of it remains which is eternal.

—Spinoza

What do we do now, now that we are happy?
—Samuel Beckett, *Waiting for Godot*

An image of scented smoke—gentle and sensual wisps, hung in air—looks like the image of bones in an X-ray film. The fair ladies in brocaded, laced, silver-frilled, white cambric dresses are so elegantly delicate that if touched hard they could metamorphose into clean water, then scatter and vanish. Their seraphic eyes are large, and their faces change with each stylistic turn of their heads, that, a moment later Muhammad Ameen cannot tell who was who. There is an abstract painting on the golden wall—studded with diamonds, emeralds and rubies—in which two lovers seem to be kissing each other but actually aren't. On a close look, it turns out to be a painting of an abstract goblet. Everything inside and outside is so perfect and absolute that he is painfully confused.

Ameen has found all the scriptural promises true and fulfilled. Here he is again—a thirty-year-old youthful, sturdy Ameen and not the man who was hit by a bullet at fourty-two. He no longer stammers; all the impediments from his tongue have been removed. And he doesn't care whether he makes sense or not. He is surrounded by the promised streams of milk and honey, large-eyed houris, 'like scattered pearls around him', and trees, heavily laden with fruits of large sizes, far-reaching scents and brash colours, and pretty birds perched on their branches, warbling sweet birdsong into the dense foliage—all that he had repeatedly heard of in his Quran lessons and Friday sermons in the worldly life. He now lives in a palatial house. He lies down on velvety divans against soft, satin-cased bolsters. There is hardly a moment when he feels alone, but slowly all these absolute pleasures are becoming a routine affair and beginning to bore him. Of course, he has already had answers to the countless complicated questions he had always suffered thinking about, and had ever waited and wanted to ask. Those questions have been answered in a language he could not have even wished to speak in, in his worldly life, but above all, he has understood the answers well and has been convinced. Ameen has met many of his relatives and friends and acquaintances who have reached here before him. He is surprised to see many of those who he or even any well-meaning person in the world had never ever, by any means, expected to make it to heaven. Yet they have. He is more surprised at not finding those who everyone, almost all the well-meaning persons in the world, had bet that they belonged in heaven. They have all died in the world, but are absent here. Without problems and with everything perfect and gratifying around him, Ameen believes that there still is but one major problem in the heaven. And that is that heaven is without problems but his mind is conscious. A conscious mind feeds on problems.

In his worldly life, Muhammad Ameen exhaustively thought about identity confrontations, race combats, communal clashes, civilizational conflicts, power tussles, oil wars and what not. He would ponder and ponder over great existential and moral questions, the questions about good and bad and their origins and ultimate purposes. Ameen was a self-styled student of philosophy. Self-styled, because each university in Kashmir had everything except a faculty of philosophy where he could have pursued the subject on post-graduation level and beyond. He had studied the subject from his higher secondary level towards the end of his college, had been guided by mediocre teachers who knew nothing about philosophy, and consequently he learnt by teaching himself and from occasional parleys with his jobless wise friends who were much elder to him.

His parents were peasants and couldn't afford a private English-medium school for him and for his three elder brothers and two younger sisters. Like his siblings, he received his primary education in an Urdu-medium government school at Natipora. In a way, Ameen was split in his day to day social dealings: Polite to polite people, aggressive to mediocre, a lover and yet a pleasant liar to his wife, a loving, caring, nagging and beating father to his two sons, a brusque and argumentative, yet a very obedient son. He felt shy of confessing his love to his parents and brothers and sisters. For he had been brought up like that. He had experienced elsewhere that many who confessed love more and more fondly actually loved less and less practically. It'd make the whole affair of love more verbal and less actual. Instead he would say things, which were opposites to those confessions. But the knowledge of any harm to his relatives would send his bowels rumbling with worry and fear. Once a doctor misdiagnosed his eldest brother with 'ulceration in the stomach', which was actually a minor case of acid reflux, and Ameen got more sickened than his brother. His brother recuperated, but, himself, Ameen dehydrated in depression.

Once in a dream, he saw his mother dying and then that whole day, after waking up from the dream, he furtively cried in the attic. In soliloquy he told himself he could not live without her and for that matter if he had to die, he should die before her. In his high school days, Ameen read about Socrates, Plato and Aristotle. He developed an interest in philosophy and it only grew and grew. Later he would study all the great minds he came across, borrowing their books from his friends and libraries, and sometimes not returning them. He learnt that Louis Althusser, the German philosopher, often lost in a stupor of thought, once while massaging his wife's neck, unknowingly strangled her to death and later the court too acquitted him for her 'murder', accepting that the philosopher had done so unintentionally in a certain mental condition. Ameen disliked such extremities. He also despised the fact that Saul Bellow would be so absorbed in his literary work that his wife and their son had to seek appointments to see him. But still, despite hating such extremities, Ameen himself, easily tended to give into them.

During his college years, Ameen also doubled as a teacher in various private schools, teaching social sciences to high school kids. The principals of these schools often received complaints from their students that Ameen frequently deviated from the topic and lapsed into philosophizing history and politics. Something that was heavy for the school-going students to understand and digest. He would habitually leave the syllabus unfinished because he spent a long time 'intellectualizing' the lessons. By the end of his college, Ameen had passionately and enthusiastically studied almost all the great schools of thought and all the isms. He developed his own notion of looking at life in the world and called his philosophy *critical responsibilism*. He believed in acts and deeds that were balanced on both belief in God and an unceasing reason to constantly, crazily and critically evaluate the belief and his existence in the world. In the long, informal, late-night shopfront debates with his elderly friends about existence in the world full of alternating, though disproportionate, suffering and happiness, he maintained 'it's what it's'. And for all the great possibilities of and imaginations about a better afterlife, he would add to this phrase and say ... 'if it isn't then wait until it's ...' But Ameen was highly inarticulate. He stammered since his birth and could never be understood properly. He couldn't produce spontaneous explanations. He would quickly regard himself as stupid and shiver and bat his eyelids and become sad. And the outcome would be that he only ascended and progressed in the levels of wisdom and consciousness. He took unfinished thoughts and speculations as challenges. His philosophy could mostly be understood from his actions. There were some people around him who were greatly articulate, but they just waffled and seldom made sense. Of such people Ameen was dismissive. He had a mixed temperament of emotion and wisdom coupled with arrogance. But above all, in any circumstance, he was never prejudiced. If he would be angry with anyone he imagined himself in the person's place and situation and tried to understand if whether he would have felt and acted in the same manner.

For five years after college, Ameen applied for various odd jobs, which he either didn't get or didn't find fulfilling in the least. All the while he applied for posts of nursing, office attendant, a peon in the court, among many others; and to earn a little financial support for himself, he would go from door-to-door, giving private tuitions to kids from rich families. Ameen ultimately got a teacher's job in a government school where he received a good salary. And immediately his parents married him to an ordinary, semi-educated, pretty girl from the neighbourhood.

One fateful day in the year 2012, the Army picked up two young boys from Natipora. People poured out onto the streets to protest, demanding release of the boys. Ameen watched the scene from the window of his bedroom, overlooking the main road of the neighbourhood. As the crowd grew thicker and the protests louder, the Army fired aerial shots to disperse the people. Ameen nimbly withdrew from the window, pulling it shut. And as soon as he turned away, a stray bullet from nowhere came piercing through the windowpane and sank into his back, touching his spine. Ameen fell.

Gradually, now he has begun to look for imperfections in the heavenly things about which he had in his worldly life always 'problematized and intellectualized'. Also, no news comes from the world, and that makes him further curious. He is dying to know what has happened to the unfinished business of wars on the earth. What has become of the game of thrones? What has come out of all the confrontations, all the anxiety, all the frustration and all the hate in the world? ... He is dying for an update ... Has Kashmir won its freedom by now? Who is the superpower now in the world? What has happened to the Middle-East finally? And if, for an example's sake, one has to die even in heaven, can he be expected to die in peace, knowing that finally the nuclear weapons have never been used, however, they have been left to rot and rust disused, wherever they were preserved in the world? And whether it has by now been realized on earth that race and caste and creed were the greatest illusive constructs that so many had so foolishly nursed and so fondly harboured? And whether people have by now understood that they are going to be accountable only for their deeds based on their knowledge and not on the basis of interferences in others' lives, nor on the basis of unknowability? Or whether they still continue to fool themselves. Each time he thinks about these issues, he is doped with pleasure. He is torn between bliss and consciousness. But everything he sees here is unquestionably perfect and absolute. After looking at the face of a houri, he cannot think about any better match. He is reminded of Hegel's 'absolute reality'. A houri's face is beyond all the beauty and charm produced after the total beauty of the entire universe were to be concentrated into a single face.

His intellect has become a reason for his suffering in heaven, hence a problem, so he has begun to think about this single problem. *What is the purpose of the mind in heaven? Is it needed here? If yes, then why has it not been limited to only appreciate the perfection and absoluteness? Or has it been?* Or could he be allowed to ask: *what the hell is heaven actually?* He thinks and thinks and is bored and perturbed.

The only alternative to his boredom is hell, but that in no case is an option. Though it is a place full of treasures of problems and imperfections, but the problem is that, in contrast to the constant pleasures in heaven, hell is full of constant suffering. Constant, absolute, perfect suffering and misery wouldn't at least let anyone find a moment's rest to think, not to speak of thinking at leisure.

An angel appears in Muhammad Ameen's palatial house in heaven as he prepares himself to make love to an indescribably pretty houri. He is curious to remove the silken cloth, glittering with its sequins of gold and precious emeralds, and unveil a platter the angel has brought. The houri waits as Ameen fights his urge to ask the angel if it could bring him a list of problems instead. Problems from anywhere in the universe—for example, somewhere a certain race of unknown aliens would have illegally occupied a planet of some other race—are most welcome. That somewhere there is some resistance war going on. Or even problems from some corner of the heaven itself where a certain group of *jannatis*, dwellers of the heaven, are complaining about the small size of grapes in their vineyards or the small size of seeds in their pomegranates. Or maybe certain streams of milk and honey have begun to dry up and there is a little crisis there. Or some *jannati* has been grievous ever since his entry into heaven for he has been demanding a dark-skinned houri, but due to the unavailability of such a creature here, as only the fair-skinned ones have been promised in heaven for *jannatis*, he has suffered at the cost of this *small* unfulfilled desire. Anything can do; something that he needs to think over. But such problems have never been reported to occur in heaven. Everyone here is content with what one has been blessed and bestowed with. But then he is yet to know if any of the *jannatis* he knows has the same complaint and the same problem as his, that of what to think about in heaven and why? *Is there any social contract on indifference among the jannatis? Are all jannatis bestowed with equal levels of consciousness here? And what kind of consciousness? Does eternal stay in heaven only suit indifferent hedonists?* And he literally swallows his tongue while resisting asking such blasphemous and stupid questions. But he tries to please the angel in order to create possibilities for asking such questions in future. As soon as Ameen begins to dust off the tip of the angel's left wing a speck of silver dust that he has just spotted, his hand is stopped and he is informed by a certain voice that while travelling towards him through the cosmos, the angel accidentally brushed a galaxy on its way and there is no need to dust its wing as it is going to refix the cosmic thing to its position in the universe. The angel has to travel back, half a million light years, to carry out the task which wouldn't take it more than half a second or so. This arresting learning leaves Ameen's mouth agape. And he now thinks that he should ask his favourite questions about the universe, that have always lurked in him, of the angel. *What is vacuum, that surrounds universe, actually made of? And, in fact, what was vacuum originally? And if it was nothingness, then how far did that nothingness spread? Did it have its own infinity? If yes, then what would the place where it met with the universe be called?*

He thinks of Spinoza's 'conceptions of self and universe' ... *When the mind imagines its own lack of power, it is saddened by it ...*

But he cannot ask any such questions, which can become a reason for his exit from the heaven like Adam. Thinking of Adam, he cannot now resist his temptation to think about finding the exact place where his forefather had eaten the forbidden fruit of wheat. Ameen still can't do anything. He knows that each atom of his existence in heaven is being watched by God, who is utterly pleased with him and will not chastise him for merely harbouring such intentions. God instead rewards people for good intentions. Muhammad Ameen keeps quiet about his problems. And wishes that he were in a place where there was no heaven and no hell, not even the knowledge of self; a place of no existence, a place of no questions and no answers, no pain, no rewards, nothing; a place of complete silence and unknowingness, unconsciousness—all like a dreamless sleep ... But the value of the pleasure of being in such place could only be known in consciousness.

... *What is the purpose of the mind in heaven?* Ameen murmured the same question again and again. The murmurs grew louder and louder. And he began to stammer. Sweating, he woke up to find his mother beside him, comforting him, trying to wake him up already, trying to hold away his hands from his throat—as he would often try to strangle himself in sleep—fanning away the flies that bumbled round and round in the room for sometime and then returned and landed on his face again. Ameen lay steady in his bed, frail to lapse into one more long, deep slumber.

Doctors had decided not to take any chance with the surgery on Ameen's back. Removing the bullet, they believed, could paralyse his whole body or might even lead to his death. He was prescribed medicines that were expected to dissolve the bullet to an extent. And that would take a long time.

Muhammad Ameen has been in bed, lying on his back for a year now, staring at his monthly X-ray films and reports, trying to trace the position and size of the silent bullet.

The Woman Who Became Her Own Husband

Can you be one and the same person at the same time? ... Maybe a person gets better by just letting herself be who she is.

—Ingmar Bergman, *Persona*

In my life nothing of the sort happened that, I can say, was unusual or was something that might not have happened to you—except the tale I am going to tell.

In the early '90s, when I used to run a grocery store in the neighbourhood, a new family arrived to rent the vacant first floor in the popular Khan Sojourn at Jawahar Nagar. The Sojourn was across the link road, exactly opposite my shop. In the vicinity of the Lal Chowk market hub of Srinagar city, Jawahar Nagar was one of the buzzing neighbourhoods where people from farther villages of Kashmir would come to take refuge as tenants. The insurgency movement was more active in villages and the people would frequently become targets of Army retaliations. The situation was no good in the city either, but since the city was always on the media radar, and above all it was the city, it attracted students, government employees, blacklisted politicians, and even the 'wanted' insurgents from the villages.

I was, I must say, the famed local guide to people seeking houses on rent. I kept the update on all the relinquishments and 'to-lets'. I knew the rent details, variable facilities, advantages, agreement policies and the temperaments of the owners. I was the trusted custodian of the neighbourhood. So I even kept keys of certain flats, of big houses like Yousuf Villa, Bhat Cottage, Khan Sojourn and many more. Almost all the flat owners and tenants were my regular customers. Some tenants would stay for years, some for several months, some just for a few. Some would vacate their flats without notice and become my absconding debtors for the grocery they would take on credit. I'd become family friends with many of them. Many friendships lasted even years after the tenants were gone. Some grew so attached to my family that now they are the only people who frequently travel down to the city to pay visits to me and my bedridden wife. But of them all, the tenant family I remember the most is the Zargars.

There were only three persons in the Zargar family: Tariq Zargar, his wife Ayesha and his old mother whose name I didn't know, except the fact that everyone called her Aaapa Ji. Tariq and Ayesha, as I gradually learnt, were married for five years and still trying for a child. The Zargars took the first floor in the Khan Sojourn. I don't exactly remember whether it was 1991 or 1992, but only that it was a certain year in the early '90s and the month was February.

Tariq Zargar was a handsome man of medium height and moderate build. He had a sallow face with a smart-looking shot of well-trimmed, boxed beard and his hair parted on a side. It took me a month to notice that he had a congenital defect in his right foot. In order to lift that leg to walk, he had to give a slight flick to it. Yet his pleasant personality overshadowed this small. The most memorable thing about Tariq was not his defective foot but a lively smile he always wore. Tariq was a manager in the Jammu & Kashmir Bank. He had shifted from his native village in south Kashmir's Islamabad district to Jawahar Nagar, pursuant to his transfer which, to get rid of the volatile situation in his hometown, he had himself volunteered for. He was posted in the Lal Chowk branch of the bank.

Ayesha was a pretty, fair woman, modest and modern and educated. She had lost both her parents in a road accident much before her marriage to Tariq. Her younger sister lived in south Kashmir and was married to a local contractor who lately had lost work to the volatile situation in the village. Soon after his marriage to Ayesha, Tariq's father had passed away of lung cancer. His two elder brothers had renounced him and their mother. The most interesting thing about Tariq and Ayesha was that their marriage had been an arranged one and despite the fact, they loved each other as if they had been in love since childhood. Ayesha was a homemaker.

It took the Zargars only a few days to gel with me. Tariq would address me as Haji saeb, even when I hadn't yet gone for Haj, the pilgrimage to Mecca. Each time he came down for candles or curd or biscuits or bread or eggs or cigarettes, we chatted about the turmoil in his village and the situation in the city.

My shop faced the verandah of the flat the Zargars had put up in. I observed their movements and came to understand that Tariq and Ayesha were an ideal couple. I had never known as lovely a husband-wife pair as them. With time I was convinced that in that entire neighbourhood, they were an epitome of love. And eventually, the couples among the neighbours and the tenants living on the ground and second floors of Khan Sojourn would in their occasional trifles and family squabbles often refer to Tariq and Ayesha to cite examples of love to each other.

Ayesha regarded me as a father figure and respected me more than my own children did. Early each morning, she would come out on the verandah, lean over the rail topping the grille along its verge, and greet me with a salaam and ask me about my and my family's well-being. Then she would squat on the verandah, polishing her husband's black brogues, slant the shoes against the wall in a patch of sunlight to shine. And Tariq would sit in a basket chair—the upper half of his body hidden behind an Urdu newspaper—smoking his morning cigarettes, rustling the paper every now and then, turning the pages, his legs crossing each other. Minutes later, sounds of clanking ladles, sizzling skillets and hissing pressure cookers would come from the gauze door of their kitchen.

The smell of fizzling omelettes would waft across the road and reach my shop. An hour later, she would again arrive on the verandah and give one more hard burnish to the sun-glazed shoes. Dressed mostly in a navy blue suit, carrying a briefcase, Tariq would emerge, ready to leave for office. She would help him with his shoes and he would always withdraw and insist that he do the laces himself and that she shouldn't spoil him like that. But she wouldn't listen to him and continued with the laces, and all the while he would try to pull his feet away and laugh, and she would laugh back, as if it were a game of tie-my-laces-if-you-can, and she would hold one of his legs, pinch its calf and laugh again, send him screaming and hold the leg steady in the crook of her arm, and he would give up and laugh again.

While dusting the shop, stacking the bricks of bread loaves into a block on the front counter and hanging the net baskets, full of packets of potato chips, on the hooks outside the shop for better display, I'd furtively notice these sweet exchanges between Tariq and Ayesha almost every day. And as soon as they became conscious of my presence, the couple would shyly pull themselves together and donned a serious demeanour. Ayesha would rearrange her dupatta and Tariq would clear his throat, and both would regard me respectfully with the loveliest of smiles. Long after he would disappear at the turn off on the link road and take the main road, she would look fixedly at him. Most often he would forget his wallet and she would loudly call out to me from the verandah and request me to stop him with my finger whistle. He would be about to disappear at the turn off, but he'd stop. She would run out barefooted with his wallet. I'd envy their love and narrate it every day to my wife, expecting to convert her. But nothing would change her and she would still be the same as she always was grumpy. If I forgot my credits' account ledger sometimes while leaving for the shop in the morning, my wife would curse my poor memory and endlessly nag me once I'd return home in the evening.

Ayesha's mother-in-law preferred to live indoors. I rarely saw her come out on the verandah. She would sit in the basket chair for some five minutes or so and slip back into the flat. Around noontime, after spreading Tariq's washed laundry on the clothesline strung across the verandah, Ayesha would come to my shop to buy vegetables. Every day she would choose a different variety, but potatoes were be a daily affair. 'Whatever the main dish for dinner, but Tariq saeb has to have French fries. He loves them,' she would say, picking and choosing the fresh ones.

On certain evenings, Tariq returned carrying plastic bags full of gifts for his wife and his mother. Probably clothes or shoes. Yet before entering Khan Sojourn gates, he would come straight to the shop for his pack of cigarettes. He would also ask for a dozen unwrapped *khoya* lozenges made from milk and coconut. 'Ayesha is crazy about them,' he would say shyly, while taking out the lozenges from the jar on the counter.

One day there was no movement on the verandah, no sounds or smells of cooking came out. I grew curious, and after waiting till afternoon, I worried so much that I pulled the shutter half down and went into Khan Sojourn. I found Ayesha ill, bedridden and restless with high fever. Tariq was dabbing her forehead with a wet cloth, trying to subdue the fever. And the little time I stayed beside her bed solacing her, I heard Tariq countlessly saying *bala'i lagai* (may your illness shift to me) or *zuv wandai* (may my life shield you against illness) to her. And each time, she would feebly and shyly respond with 'don't say that'. I envied this too. Never in my life had my wife said such things to me. Never had she responded to my '*bala'i lagai*', however, shyly I had tried to say it to her. Whenever I caught a cold or something, she would blame me for the illness, rather accuse me of being careless with weather; she would curse me for not taking necessary precautions. I would feel more unwell by her constant taunts than by my illness.

One more interesting thing about the couple was that they responded to anyone's question or query in unison. Both spoke at same time with similar response or answer or opinion or solution, same set of words, same syntaxes in their sentences, and in a similar tone and tenor. It was surprising to see, that though spontaneous, how perfectly matched their thinking was, how perfect the timing of the delivery of their words, how coincidentally their minds worked: simultaneous bargain rates proposed to vendors of blankets; same complaint to the milkman for adding water to milk; equal questions to me, enquiring after my and my family's well-being.

These things and many more made Tariq and Ayesha an extraordinary couple. Yet fate didn't seem to like the love between the husband and the wife.

※

Lately Srinagar had grown intensely turbulent. Day in and day out there were curfews, shutdowns and crossfires between the troops and the insurgents. Many men from Jawahar Nagar had shops or business establishments at Lal Chowk. Offices of several others were situated around the place. One day the neighbourhood folks returned early to their homes from work. They stopped at my shop to tell me that there had been a severe gunfight on Residency Road in Srinagar.

On the verandah, at that unusual hour for people to return home from work, Ayesha too stood, expecting her husband early. Tariq didn't turn up. As it grew dark, and Ayesha could no longer bear pacing the verandah while waiting for her husband, she came downstairs, her right shoe in the left foot and vice versa. Impatient, she stood outside Khan Sojourn, steadily gazing at the turn off and wringing her hands in restlessness. It grew darker. I shut my shop and joined her at the Sojourn gate, consoling her, and assuring her that her husband was on his way home and he would arrive any minute. Soon, she began enquiring about Tariq's whereabouts with the returning neighbours. They said that they hadn't seen him. Moments later, she started asking every unknown passerby about Tariq. I repeated the question each time she asked a stranger about her husband. I did it in order to make it known to the people that she was really worried and not odd. In the greyish darkness, I could not see her anxious face properly, but as a figure in the night she looked gaunt and attenuated. She seemed bereft and cold. I just kept consoling her and promising that Tariq would return. Her eyes were fixed on the turn-off, apparently set on an imaginary, empty shadowy figure in which Tariq was going to appear any second. The shadowy figure remained still empty.

It was quarter to ten in the night, I remember, and the last remnants of returnees were passing, talking about civilian casualties at Lal Chowk. Now she didn't dare ask any details of any passerby. By now two ladies from the other flats of Khan Sojourn and my wife had joined us in solidarity. It was so cold outside that Ayesha's teeth would sometimes chatter while talking. Tariq's mother was silently kneeling over the grille of the verandah. She was well aware of the situation, but vaguely enough not once did she ask us anything. When she was tired of leaning, she sat down on the edge of the verandah, coughing incessantly, intently looking in our direction through her glasses. We could later see only her silhouette there.

My wife went over to Tariq's mother to console her. And one of the ladies fetched Ayesha's shawl. I cued her to correct her shoes. In a matter of moments, the three of us, Ayesha, the lady who lived on the ground floor of

Khan Sojourn, and I, set out, piercing the pitch-dark cloth of the night with a sharp shaft of torchlight, towards the main road, looking for Tariq. All the way, as we walked quaveringly, all that we heard was barking of dogs and nothing else. Every shop was shuttered, each gate was locked, each house blacked out, each window shut. At a few places, one could only hear a faint hum of families coming from the windows of houses which were close to the main road. To reach Tariq's office, the Jammu & Kashmir Bank, on Residency Road, we had to cross the Jhelum by boat. And finding a boat at that hour was dead impossible. The river flowed gently near Lal Mandi, the ghat where in daytime boats could be hired to ferry you across. It became impossible to take the longer route because Zero Bridge was very far from Lal Mandi and at that late hour, in that situation in the city, it was very risky too. Another way through Amira Kadal Bridge was the most dangerous. There were several bunkers on the way to Amira Kadal and the biggest of them all was on the bridge itself. We promised Ayesha that we would try again the next morning. I persuaded her, saying that Tariq might have taken refuge somewhere after the encounter. She was reluctant to return home, worry had singed her face. But somehow we managed to take her back to Khan Sojourn. That whole night, my wife and the two neighbourhood ladies stayed back, consoling Ayesha. I returned home. It was just half a dozen houses away from my shop.

Early next morning, the neighbourhood was yet to come to life, when two men on a motorcycle arrived at Khan Sojourn. I was at the gate and the women, leaning over the handrail of the verandah, were intently peeking from above. In a very low voice that couldn't reach the women, the men asked if anyone by the name of Tariq Zargar lived there. The daunting way this question was asked made my hamstrings melt, and I felt I was crumbling like some fragile tower. A certain spasmodic bowel movement surged up and receded down to the last bit of my gut. I replied in affirmative. The men wanted me to accompany them. Gauging the urgency of the moment, I straddled behind them on the edge of the seat, leaving trails of doubt and uncertainty for the women on the verandah. My heart swelled with foreboding.

As the bike whooshed on the main road, a nippy wind began to take my voice away. The cold wind stung my eyes. It began to dry my face up. Two trails of already drying tears streamed towards my temples, defying gravity in the wind. Tariq was no more, the men announced and quietly rendered me to chew my lips behind them and wince.

The men surmised that Tariq had just left office when the bunker outside it was attacked, and of all the passersby present around, he was the only one unable to run for his life. The only person on my mind now was Ayesha. Not Tariq. He quickly faded out of my mind with the news of his death. The only thought nagging at me was a question: what will she do now?

Soon I found myself in the small, mud-plastered mortuary of the Srinagar Police Control Room.

Tariq looked like he were sleeping. His well-ironed, striped grey suit had absorbed the blood that had oozed out of his body. Both his legs had bullets in them and one had sunk into his neck. I signed some paper and immediately took charge of the body. It was placed in a large blue police truck. As the truck neared its destination, my gut began to rumble with fear. But when the chaos of a sloganeering crowd loomed in the distance, I heaved a sigh of relief. The news had already hit the neighbourhood. Khan Sojourn was abuzz with angry protestors. I thanked God for sparing me the task of being the first person to break the tragic news to the neighbourhood and above all, to Ayesha.

Ayesha drowned in a river of women. As the truck trundled, reversing close to the house, I could hear a faded wail thicken and roar at the sight of the visible dead body in the back of the truck. It took me a while to spot my wife. She seemed struggling with Ayesha who was hidden behind a wall of women. I thanked God for not being able to spot Ayesha because I didn't want to see her and I wished I hadn't known her. I imagined her in many ways. Crying or laughing or slapping herself, beating her chest, pulling her hair or shocked into silence. I couldn't see Tariq's mother at all. For sometime I had forgotten her.

I busied myself with the elders from the neighbourhood, making necessary arrangements to carry the body to

Tariq's hometown, sixty kilometres away from Srinagar.
The wails and protests grew louder each minute, and the
loudest around noon, when Tariq's brothers, their wives
and Ayesha's sister arrived. And it was then that I spotted
Ayesha. Surprisingly, she looked normal. I couldn't
believe my eyes. The neighbourhood women, my wife,
Ayesha's sister and her sisters-in-law were begging her to
cry, but she didn't react. Finally, I found Tariq's mother;
she was bareheaded, with not a trace of tear in her eyes,
but only wailing. And her wailing sounded more like
grumbling. There was a fresh wound on her forehead, a
slanting slash surrounded by a crust of gore. Perhaps she
had banged her head against something hard and sharp.
Women were applying turmeric paste to her forehead.

Later that afternoon, quickly after the *zuhar* prayer,
a caravan of small trucks and buses was loaded with
mourners, supporting neighbours and Tariq's body, and
flagged off to Islamabad. We reached in the evening
and directly headed to Tariq's ancestral graveyard in
Mattan. The whole village had come down for the
funeral. Just after the burial and *fateha*, we paid a visit
to Tariq's house to assess the situation. The evening was
relentlessly turning into night. My wife and a few more
from the neighbourhood of Jawahar Nagar stayed back
with Tariq's wife and his family. Some fellows from my
neighbourhood and I returned home around midnight,
crossing a dozen identification parades on the way. There
was no cell phone then and landline, too, was rare, so I
couldn't inform my wife about my reaching back safely.

Early next morning, I made another long journey to pay a visit to Tariq's bereaved family. All the way, in my mind, I turned over a load of many memories of Tariq and Ayesha.

This time I could see Ayesha closely, yet I couldn't dare say a word of consolation. She looked normal as usual, but completely silent. I could only put my hand on her head and she didn't even glance at me. Tariq's mother was still grumbling tearlessly and the wound on her head was now an angry clot. A sing-song dirge continuously resonated in the house full of mourners. A hall was packed with Tariq's friends and colleagues from the bank. Later that afternoon, my wife and I returned to Srinagar, not speaking a word but heaving deep sighs all the way.

The locked flat in Khan Sojourn, its barren verandah and the potatoes and *khoya* lozenges in my shop began to haunt me. The whole neighbourhood in Jawahar Nagar was disturbed by Tariq's death, recounting and stoking anecdotes about the lovely relationship Tariq and Ayesha had shared. Many began to believe that their relationship was so exceptionally beautiful that it couldn't resist falling prey to an evil eye.

On the ritualistic 'fourth', and the last, day of mourning, we paid another visit to the bereaved family. This time it was strange to see Ayesha. Silent, though, she didn't stay put but paced here and there in the room, where people had come to pay condolences, limping exactly the way Tariq did. At first I thought she was relaxing a tingled leg or so. Then I thought she had injured it. But the relatives said that her leg was all right. We left, befuddled. On the way to Srinagar, my wife made several wild guesses about the limping, but we still couldn't get it.

A week later, I was surprised to see Ayesha back in her Sojourn flat. She was accompanied by her sister and a few other women I hadn't seen before. I was pleased to see her, but it was also strange to find her the same way as I had seen her on the last day of mourning. I learnt from her sister that she was still in shock, and bringing her back to Srinagar was an experiment to see if the flat and its memories would snap her out of the state. Upon hearing about Ayesha's return, gradually, the neighbours in Jawahar Nagar began to throng Khan Sojourn. But Ayesha was completely indifferent to everyone.

The next day was more astonishing than ever. She stood on the verandah, leaning on the railing over the grille the way Tariq did, smoking a cigarette exactly in his style. Standing in the same posture and in the same manner as that of Tariq, she greeted me in a man's tone. Some days later, I saw her hair cut like Tariq's. She paced the verandah, limping like Tariq. The ladies quietly watched her, crying behind her back. An hour later, she came down limping towards my shop and stood across the counter just like Tariq used to, asking for *khoya* lozenges. Taking out the lozenges from the jar on the counter, she said shyly: 'Ayesha is crazy about them.'

The ladies in the flat tried their best to keep her indoors because day by day Ayesha was turning into a spectacle for the neighbourhood. Another day, I found her dressed in Tariq's navy-blue suit, smoking a cigarette just like him, wearing his pair of brogues, carrying his leather briefcase, limping down the lane for 'office'.

A fortnight might have passed and then one morning, while opening my shop, I found a big load carrier parked outside Khan Sojourn. I went upstairs and saw Ayesha's sister and the other women packing the belongings of Ayesha and Tariq. Two labourers were loading the items into the truck. Ayesha was inside. Her sister said that it was a coincidence that I had come to see them because she was otherwise going to come to settle the final rent and their account at my shop. I collected the rent and electricity bill and quickly left. In a few hours, the load carrier was chugging to leave. An Ambassador car had already arrived for the ladies. Ayesha's brother-in-law was sitting beside the driver. With staggering steps, I went to bid farewell to a feverish Ayesha, half dressed in Tariq's clothes, being seated in the middle of the rear seat. I couldn't say anything except praying for God's mercy on her and placing my hand on her head. Ayesha's sister extracted a promise from me of occasional visits. The flat was empty now and conversations between the labourers began to echo.

A small crowd gathered to bless Ayesha. My wife and some neighbourhood women began to sob and snivel softly.

In the last twenty-three years, my wife and I have visited Ayesha countless times in Islamabad. And on each visit, we found her dressed like Tariq, limping down the lanes, being followed by giggling and curious children. And in these twenty-three years, my wife has responded to my *bala'i lagai* without fail.

Acknowledgements

'The Gravestone' was first published in the July 2014 issue of *The Caravan* and was later anthologized in *A Clutch of Indian Masterpieces: Extraordinary Short Stories from the 19th Century to the Present* (Aleph Book Company, 2014).

'Psychosis' was first published in *Kashmir Lit* in 2013.

'Country-Capital' appeared in the *Kindle* magazine in 2013.

'The Silent Bullet' was published as 'Ameen in Heaven' in *The Byword* in its June 2015 issue.

All other stories in this collection have never been published before.